Killers
In The
Shadow

Killers In The Shadow

From the Editors
Of *True Story* And
True Confessions

Published by True Renditions, LLC

True Renditions, LLC
105 E. 34th Street, Suite 141
New York, NY 10016

ISBN: 978-1-938877-71-1

Visit us on the web at www.truerenditionsllc.com.

Contents

STALKED BY A KILLER
I have to protect myself

$\mathbf{W}$hen my soon-to-be ex-husband had told me that his new girlfriend might do me bodily harm, I hadn't believed a word that he'd said.

"You're in terrible danger," Michael warned. "Brianne might even try to kill you."

"Kill me? But that's crazy. Why would she want to kill me?" I asked, shocked

I'd stared at him in disbelief. While it was true that the times when I'd been around Brianne, she had been distant and unfriendly, I'd understood the reasons for her behavior. Michael had been very vocal about the fact that he didn't want our marriage to end. I was the one who'd thought that we'd both be better off with someone else.

Michael and I had married a couple of years earlier after my first husband, the father of my children, had been killed in a car accident. I was desperately lonely and Michael's attention had seemed to be just what I'd needed. Back in those days, I'd thought that his dramatic flare was exciting, but when we'd started living in the real world, his theatrics had soon grown old.

Always a "drama king," Michael had been able to turn the simplest situation into a soap opera. I'd always been the practical, down-to-earth type, and his constant hand-wringing had soon gotten tiresome.

Now, though, he was looking at me with real tears in his eyes. Desperation and actual fear were clearly written on his face. He was even wringing his hands. There was no doubt that his agitation was real, but I'd known better than to get excited. His words always could have been a trick, so that I'd let him move back in with me.

"She's obsessed with jealousy over you," Michael went on. "She raves constantly about how much she hates you."

"Did you two have another fight?" I was completely unconcerned about the so-called threats, because I didn't believe him. Michael had always exaggerated the truth.

Also, after meeting Brianne, I'd decided that she was very much like Michael in temperament. So, I'd just figured that she always overreacted, too.

"All we do is fight. I tell you, Janine, the woman is crazy. I'm scared of her. But I'm more scared for you than for me."

He'd taken a long sip of his soda, then set the cup back on the table of the fast-food restaurant where we'd met. I'd only gone to meet him because he'd insisted that it was an emergency. But Michael was in the depths of his theatrical throes, and I'd figured it was all just smoke. It would be a relief when our divorce was finalized next month.

"I don't think Brianne would hurt me," he said. "It's you that she always gets upset over. She claims that you're trying to ruin our romance. She rants and raves and keeps saying that, if you would only die, our lives would be perfect. Then she could be a mother to the children."

"Now listen, Michael," I snapped, starting to get angry. "Tell Brianne to have her own kids, because she's never getting mine!"

Michael had planned to adopt my two children, but when we'd started having trouble in our marriage, I'd put a stop to that. Sometimes, the kids still went on outings with him and Brianne. After all, he'd become fond of them, and I'd wanted to be fair.

Michael had jerked back as if I'd slapped him, and I'd felt badly. There had never been any doubt in my mind that he'd loved my kids. He'd tried to be the best father that he could to them, and he'd been devastated when I'd asked him to move out.

"I think of them as my very own," he told me. But, in spite of his good intentions, he just wasn't a very dependable person. Often, he'd promised that he'd pick up the kids for a movie or some other treat. Then, he'd fail to show up, or even to call.

"I don't want to seem callous," I said, "but I don't want to be involved in your relationship with Brianne. What goes on between the two of you is none of my business."

My kids were frolicking in the adjoining play area. I could hear Bryan's laughter and his five-year-old sister's giggles as they'd crawled through large plastic tubes. At eight, Bryan was advanced for his age, and unusually patient with Jessica.

Now that I had separated from Michael, things were going really well for the kids and me. Much better than they had while I was married to him.

It had taken Michael a while to accept the divorce, and when he'd finally begun dating Brianne, I was happy for him. She'd seemed to feed off the problems that Michael kept stirring up, so I'd figured that they were two of a kind and would get along well together. However, I'd had no desire to be part of their ongoing drama, and I'd proceeded to tell Michael that.

"Don't even mention my name to her. Stop singing my praises every minute of the day. I know how you are," I reminded him. "You probably keep comparing us."

I'd studied Michael, understanding Brianne's attraction to the

2

man. Michael was a handsome guy, good looking enough to remind you of a popular movie star. The two of them looked really good together, too. Like a matched set, I thought.

"There's no reason for Brianne to feel threatened by me," I continued. "Our marriage was over long before the two of you met."

I'd glanced at the kids again, and I was glad that they seemed to be having a great time. It was nice to sit down for a minute. I was on my feet for long hours at the discount center where I was the manager of the housewares department.

"You don't understand, Janine." Michael had leaned closer, as if someone might try to overhear our conversation. "I really think that the woman's crazy with jealousy. She wants to know where I am every minute of the day. I even had to lie to her about coming over here today."

"But that's ridiculous. I told you, I'm no threat to Brianne. Just keep me out of your lives," I insisted. I figured that, maybe, if I'd repeated the words enough times, he'd believe me. I'd glanced at my watch. It was growing late, and I still had laundry to do when I got home.

"Brianne would feel better if you were dating someone else, I think." Michael made wet circles on the table with his cup. I'd assumed that he didn't want to meet my gaze, since I was growing annoyed with the pretend crisis. "Have you met anyone special yet?" he asked.

"I'm sorry, Michael, but I can't live my life just to please your girlfriend. I'd like to meet someone, but that hasn't happened yet. You can tell her that I'm keeping my eyes open for the right guy, though." There, I thought. Maybe that will calm her down.

Finding another man wasn't something that I was worried about. My job was exciting and challenging. Also, I pitched on the church's softball team, and spent all of my spare time with my kids. The way I'd figured it, my life was happy and full. I'd meet Mr. Right sometime, but there was no hurry.

My life wasn't perfect, of course. My job required me to do difficult things. Why, just that morning, I'd had to fire an employee named Tina Runyon because she'd been caught stealing. The woman had become hysterical, and the whole scene had been pretty miserable.

Michael's anxiety over my safety wasn't making my day any easier. Suddenly, more than anything else, I'd wanted to be in my own comfortable little two-story house. I'd bought my home at a good price from an older woman who'd wanted to move into a condo. I'd fixed it up myself on my days off, and I'd wanted to be there at that very moment with my children. I'd tried to reassure Michael as best I could, and then, I'd sent him on his way. The only drama I'd wanted in my life was the kind that came from books and TV.

The following week had flown by so quickly that it almost had taken my breath away. I'd forgotten all about Michael and his dramatic concerns. But it was a fun-filled week. The church softball team had won another game, and everyone had insisted that it was because of my fast pitching. I'd tried to be modest, but to tell the truth, I was pleased with the improvement in my pitching skills. Always athletic by nature, I had worked out with weights to become even stronger. We were eligible to play in a tournament that weekend.

Mom had watched the kids while I'd played the out-of-town game that Saturday. The rest of the group had traveled to the little town of Oak View in the church van. They'd planned to attend a service before coming back, but I'd wanted to hurry home to the kids, so I'd driven my own car. I didn't get very many Saturdays off, and I didn't want to spend the whole day away from them. But I didn't mind driving home alone. We'd won again, and I was in a great mood.

A small mountain range crossed a stretch of the highway and was really lovely. I was enjoying the breathtaking view when, suddenly, I'd noticed an old, beat-up car tailgating me. I'd glanced at my instruments and noticed that I was driving the speed limit.

"Sorry," I muttered under my breath, "but you're going to have to be patient for a while. We'll come to a passing zone soon." I'd glanced into the rearview mirror and noticed that the driver wore a hat with the brim pulled down, so that shadows hid the face. I'd frowned. The driver could have been either a man or a woman. It was hard to tell. But, whoever it was, the person was going to have to cool it for a couple more miles.

Suddenly, the driver pulled into the opposite lane, and my heart leapt into my throat. What was that maniac thinking? If a car had come around the curve from the other direction, someone could have been killed—possibly me.

I'd wanted to get as far away from the person as possible, so I'd hit the brakes to let them pass. But, as soon as I'd done that, the driver of the car had braked, too.

Fear had sliced through me, and my arms and legs had felt as though they'd melted into butter. What was the person thinking? Then, suddenly, things had worsened. The driver had banged into my car and pushed me toward the cliff. My mouth went dry with unadulterated fear. I'd never been so scared in my life. Thoughts of my children, left motherless, had knifed through my heart.

"Dear God," I prayed desperately. "Please help me."

A short railing was the only thing that stood between me and a sheer drop straight down. My car had scraped against one of the stout little poles that was holding corrugated metal strips. I'd managed to keep the wheel turned sharply to the left to prevent being forced off the road. If I'd hit the metal, instead of the pole, I'd have gone right through it and sailed down the mountainside. The well-developed strength in my arms and shoulders was what had saved me.

Should I have stopped? Would that have helped? I knew, though, that the road leveled out just around the curve, and I'd decided to see if I could make it that far. If no one rounded the mountain in front of me, I might just be able to make it to safety.

Suddenly, I'd remembered my mother's parting words: "I'll pray for a safe trip," Mom had said. The phrase had seemed ordinary at the time—one of those things that she'd always said. But, suddenly, I'd desperately hoped that she had meant it. The thought of Mom's head bowed in prayer had given me the courage to keep trying.

"Help me, Lord!" I yelled, as if God might be hard of hearing.

I was driving west when the clouds overhead had suddenly drifted away, causing bright sunshine to dazzle my eyes. It must have blinded the driver in the other car, too, because, suddenly, a small amount of pressure against my fender had eased, and I was able to pull away from the railing. Just ahead, I could see what I'd been praying for. That was where the ground leveled out and the incline from the road, although steep, was something that I might be able to ride down, if, indeed, I were forced to do so.

The longest minute of my life passed as I'd pulled hard against new pressure from the car behind me. I'd thanked God for the strength in my arms. Most women wouldn't have been able to hold the car on the road.

Suddenly, the car had hit my vehicle with renewed force, and I was finally forced off the road.

Time had seemed to go in slow motion, but, somehow, I'd managed to guide the car down the steep incline.

"Oh, no! I'm going to roll over!" I shouted.

But, to my amazement, I didn't. Somehow, my dependable car had held its balance, and when the long descent had ended, I was still sitting upright in an almost-dry creek bed.

My whole body was shaking so hard that I couldn't even unfasten my seat belt. I'd just sat there, with tears running down my face.

"Thank-you, Lord," I whispered, over and over.

Then I'd seen a figure half tumble, half walk, down the incline toward me. I was startled.

The maniac must be coming down the mountain after me! I thought. I'd covered my face with my hands and begun to scream.

Finally, a voice had found its way through my cries. "Lady, don't be scared," a man's voice said. "I'm not going to hurt you. I came down to help."

I looked up to see a man peering into my window.

"I saw that car force you off the road up there, and I came to help," he told me.

The man had kept talking while I'd tried to pull myself together. Somehow, I'd managed to stop shaking long enough to unfasten my seat belt and push the release button on the door locks. Then, the man had pulled open my door and was helping me out of the car.

"I tried to get the license plate number of the other driver, but there was mud smeared all over it," the man told me. "Who would do such a thing?"

My legs were so weak that I wasn't sure if they would hold me up.

"Thanks for helping me," I whispered. My voice was hoarse as I'd looked gratefully at the man's face.

"I was behind the two of you," he explained. "I wanted to help, but I couldn't think of a thing to do. My wife had taken our cell phone with her when she went to town to buy groceries. I was helpless."

The kindly man had helped me back up to the road then, and I'd calmed down long enough to remember that my own phone was clipped to my belt. Then I'd called the highway patrol. He'd waited with me until the authorities had arrived, and I was grateful for his company.

Someone tried to kill me! That thought was a silent scream inside my head, and it turned my blood to ice water.

Even though I was almost wild with terror, I'd managed to answer all of the officer's questions. The man had told the officer what he'd seen, too, but neither of us knew much. An old car had pulled up beside me and tried to force my car down the side of a cliff. If the terrain hadn't changed when it had, and my car hadn't managed to stay upright on the wild ride down the ravine, I'd be dead, or, at best, seriously hurt.

"You did a good job of controlling that car," the man said. "You sure impressed me."

"You were lucky," the officer told me.

"Why would anyone try to kill me?" I asked. Then, suddenly, I'd remembered what Michael had said about Brianne. Could she really have been the person in the car? Did she want me dead, like Michael had said? It had all seemed like a bad dream.

"It was probably road rage," the officer commented. "You must have done something that made that driver angry. Had you just passed that car?"

"No, I didn't do anything," I insisted. "I was just driving down the road. How could such a thing have happened?"

"Who knows? Maybe they wanted to pass you, and couldn't,"

the patrolman told me. "With some folks, it doesn't take much. I'll file a report, but without the plate number, or some special description of the car or driver, there's not much hope. I'm afraid that there are a lot of older cars on the road." Then, he'd frowned. "Is there someone who might want to harm you?"

It was a minute before I'd answered. I'd hated to mention Brianne without any definite proof, but I had two kids to consider.

"My soon-to-be ex-husband has a girlfriend who doesn't like me very much," I admitted. "He warned me that she might try to harm me."

He'd made a note of that in his notebook, asking for Brianne's full name and address. But I could tell by the expression on his face that he wasn't too impressed with what I'd said. And, suddenly, I'd felt a little silly for even mentioning it.

"And she drives an old car?" the patrolman asked.

"No, actually, I think she drives a newer-model car. But I suppose she could have borrowed a car from someone else." I'd shot a quick look at the man who'd helped me, and I'd noticed that he, too, looked surprised. I'd felt myself blushing.

I'd had to admit the idea seemed a little unlikely. The thought that Brianne would track me to Oak View, and then try to kill me by running my car off the road with a borrowed car, was ridiculous. I was starting to sound just like Michael. And these two men were looking at me as if I were a hysterical female. I'd taken a deep breath and tried to relax. Maybe the officer was right—it could have been an isolated case of road rage.

I'd called Mom and told her that I'd be late. Then, I'd called the automobile club and arranged for my car to be towed to a garage. I'd gone back to town with the truck.

Luckily, I had good insurance and soon, I was driving a rental car while mine was being fixed. There hadn't been as much damage as I'd initially feared. Mostly, I'd been grateful that I hadn't been hurt. My only injury was an awful soreness over my whole body. It was as if I'd exercised too much. And I'd remembered to thank Mom for her prayers.

"I always pray for you," she told me with her sweet smile. I'd had to blink back the tears that were suddenly stinging my eyes.

I'd always bounced back from things pretty quickly, and so, in a few days, things were pretty much back to normal. That was why it had taken me completely by surprise when I'd come home one evening and found that my house had been trashed.

The kids and I had gone to see the latest animated movie, and Bryan and Jessica were still chattering excitedly over the antics of the zany characters. I'd unlocked the front door and walked inside.

Suddenly, I'd stopped, frozen in terror. My normally neat house was turned upside down, with things thrown everywhere. Some evil person had vandalized my house. Were they still there?

My first concern was for the children, so I'd swept up Jessica off her feet, grabbed Bryan's hand, and backed out the door, before they could see the mess.

"What's wrong, Mommy?" Bryan asked. "Why are we leaving? We just got here."

My heart was in my throat, but I didn't want to scare the kids by letting them know that I was afraid.

"Let's get the mail," I suggested.

"But I thought we'd already picked it up," Bryan told me. However, by that time, we were already outside.

"We're going next door to see Mrs. Lawsen," I said, as casually as I could. "Let's race and see who can get there first." I'd set Jessica on the ground, and the three of us had run to our neighbor's house as quickly as we could.

"I won! I won!" Bryan yelled, pleased with himself. Then, when he saw me ringing the bell, he'd frowned. "That's my job, Mom. I always ring the bell."

And, when I'd kept punching the bell, he'd corrected me.

"That's rude, Mom. You told me to always ring only once, and then, to give people time to get to the door. Mrs. Lawsen is elderly. Don't you remember?"

But, by that time, Mrs. Lawsen had already opened the door and was greeting us with a big smile. I'd hustled the kids inside and explained to my neighbor that our house had been broken into.

"Why, I never saw anyone go near your place," Mrs. Lawsen said, with a surprised look. "Of course, I've been inside most of the evening. Did they take much?"

"I don't know. I wanted to get the kids out of danger before I called the police." I took my cell phone out of my purse and dialed 911.

It had seemed to take forever for the police officer to reach the house. Mrs. Lawsen had settled the kids in front of the TV and turned on their favorite cartoon channel. Then, she'd served me a cup of coffee. I'd tried to drink some to be polite, but I couldn't seem to swallow.

When the doorbell had rung, I'd sighed with relief. I'd checked through the window to make sure the person was wearing a uniform. Then, I'd opened the door.

After telling the officer what little I knew about the break-in, he'd gone to check my house. I'd followed him out onto Mrs. Lawsen's porch. The policeman had stopped for a minute to reassure me.

"These break-ins are usually just smash-and-grab burglaries. A

8

thief checks the house, determines that no one is home, then takes jewelry and other items that can be turned into quick cash. I'm certain that the thief is already gone, but I'll check, anyway, just to be sure." Then he'd walked toward my house.

I'd stood on the porch and waited. The officer was gone for about five minutes. He'd come out with a perplexed look on his face.

"I was right—the place is empty. If you'd like, you can come on over."

I'd followed him back and gone inside. The destruction had made me heartsick. I'd never been burglarized before, and the viciousness of the attack had shocked me. My house had been more than robbed— it had been pulverized.

"Oh, dear God," I said sorrowfully. "This is awful!"

I'd wanted to weep. Pictures had been pulled off the walls and smashed into bits on the floor. The sofa and matching chairs were ripped, and the stuffing had been pulled out. Books had pages torn out of them. But, worst of all were my photographs. The frames had all been smashed, and the pictures ripped out and torn apart. I'd looked at the cruel destruction, sick with disappointment. My whole body was trembling with anger.

"I've never seen such wreckage," Officer Carruthers told me. "I can't understand it. Usually, these burglaries are done by people wanting quick money to buy drugs. They get in, and then, they head right back out. They don't want to spend this kind of time. It increases the risk of being caught." He'd looked around my home, shaking his head. "The kitchen is really bad," he added.

I hardly could bear to look, but I'd steeled myself and walked into the kitchen to see what I was facing. Jars and bottles had been opened and their contents poured on the counters and floors. I'd seen molasses, ketchup, honey, and mustard smeared all over my kitchen. I was so upset that I'd thought I might throw up. What would the kids think when they saw this? And, how would I ever get the mess cleaned up?

I'd walked through the rest of the house with tears rolling down my cheeks. My bedroom and the dining area looked pretty much like the living room. The only rooms that hadn't been touched were the kids' rooms.

"Whoever it was, must have run out of time," Officer Carruthers commented. "Why don't you check around and see what's missing?"

That had taken quite a while. It was hard to determine for sure what might have been missing, with things in such a mess. I couldn't find my jewelry box, or the VCR, or a small TV that I'd had in my bedroom. Those were the only things that I'd known for sure were missing.

9

I'd called Mom while Officer Carruthers had checked for fingerprints. I supposed he'd made the effort because he'd felt sorry for me, and he'd wanted me to feel as though he was doing all that he could. He did tell me not to expect too much from his effort, though. Then, he'd looked through the house again.

"Are you sure that you didn't leave a door or window open?" he asked again. "There doesn't seem to be any forced entry."

Did Brianne steal Michael's key? I thought, remembering suddenly that I had never asked to have it back.

I'd told Officer Carruthers about Brianne's threats. I'd also explained about what had happened when I'd almost been forced off the road. He'd written all of that down in his report, but I could tell from the expression on his face that I had suddenly lost his sympathy.

"These domestic disputes are always a mess," he mumbled, shaking his head. "Even if I find some of her fingerprints in your house, there's no way to prove that they weren't made at a prior time." He'd looked up at me. "I'm assuming that she's been in your house before?"

I'd thought back, trying to remember. "She came once with my ex-husband when he picked up the kids for an outing," I told him. "I think she asked to use the bathroom."

Officer Carruthers just shook his head.

Tears were flowing down my cheeks. I knew that I'd never feel safe in my house again.

The evil intruder who'd vandalized my house had caused me much grief. Being burglarized was a bit like being violated. A stranger had forced his or her way into the sanctity of my home and desecrated the place. The most precious thing that they had stolen from me was the feeling of being safe in my own house. That had seemed to be gone forever.

Mom had tried to talk me into moving in with her permanently, but I was determined not to give in to my fear. No way was anyone going to force me out of my own house. Such a thing was unthinkable. So, after spending that first night with Mom, we'd gone back home.

It had taken most of the week to clean my house. I'd fixed things as best as I could, and then, I'd thrown a couple of blankets over the ruined furniture. Mom had pitched in and helped.

"Just be glad that no one was here when that awful person came," Mom told me. And, of course, I knew that she was right. But, I'd still cried over my ruined photographs. Some things just couldn't be replaced.

The kids were traumatized, too. Bryan had nightmares, and both he and Jessica had started wanting to sleep with me. I'd decided to let them, at least for a while. That way, I'd felt as though I could protect them.

The day after the break-in, I had called Michael from work and told him what had happened.

"Do you want me to move back in for a while?" he asked.

I didn't say anything, so Michael had just kept talking.

"Just until you feel safe again," he went on. "I'm really worried about the kids."

"That wouldn't be a good idea," I assured him. "We'll be okay." I'd cleared my throat, then told him the rest. "The police will come by and talk to Brianne. Maybe that'll put the fear into her, and she'll quit harassing me."

There was a long silence. I'd thought that maybe he'd hung up.

"Hello," I said. "Michael? Are you still there?"

Finally, he'd spoken.

"Brianne couldn't have been involved," he said in a troubled voice. "She was with me all day yesterday."

I'd felt as though all of the air had left my lungs, leaving me breathless. If it hadn't been Brianne, who could it have been?

I'd realized then that maybe the two things weren't connected at all, and the break-in was just a bunch of kids, like the police officer had first thought. Or, maybe Brianne had gotten one of her low-life friends to tear up my house. Finally, I was able to speak again.

"What about that Saturday when my car was forced off the road?" I asked.

"I don't know about that. I told you she was dangerous, remember?" Then I'd heard the sound of a door slamming over the line. "Sorry, Janine, but I've got to hang up. Brianne just came home." He'd sounded frightened, and that had worried me.

"Michael, has Brianne threatened you?" I asked.

There was another long silence. "Don't worry about me," he told me finally. "I've got to go now. Good-bye." Then he hung up.

I didn't want to make trouble for Michael, but it just wasn't my nature to let things fall in on me. I'd always been sort of a face-the-problem kind of woman, and I'd intended to check out my suspicions. If the police wouldn't investigate, then I would.

And so, after work, while the kids were still at Mom's, I'd decided to drive by their apartment and have a little chat with Brianne. I'd known that Michael would be at work.

Brianne's eyes had widened when she'd answered her door and seen me standing there.

"What are you doing here?" she asked angrily.

I'd decided that there wasn't much point in mincing words.

"Did you try to force my car off the road last Saturday?" I asked.

Brianne's face had turned red, and her eyes had shot daggers at me.

11

"No, I didn't. And I don't appreciate your giving my name and address to the police," she snapped. "It was very embarrassing when they came around, asking questions. The neighbors have looked at me strangely ever since, and that's not the least bit funny."

Her attitude had ticked me off, and I'd lost my temper.

"Someone vandalized my house, stole my jewelry, and ruined my photographs, and I don't think that's funny, either," I retorted. "They tore up the whole house, except for the kids' rooms. If you're responsible for these things, I want it to stop! Right now!"

"You must be crazy, trying to accuse me like this!" Brianne yelled. Her eyes were wild looking, and just the expression in them was enough to make me take a step backward.

"You'd better watch out, or I'll have the police take those kids away from you," she went on. "They'd be much better off with Michael and me. If you're not careful, one of these days, I'll just come and get them." Then she'd slammed the door in my face.

I'd stood in the doorway, stunned by shock and shaking with anger. What on earth was she talking about? I couldn't believe that she'd just threatened to steal my kids!

A sense of fear had rippled through me and wild thoughts had begun to torment my mind. Could that have been her plan? Had she wanted to get me so stirred up that I'd do a bunch of foolish things, trying to stop the problem? Maybe she'd thought that, if I'd seemed unstable, Michael might somehow still have been able to adopt the kids. But that was just plain crazy.

I'd realized then that it had been a big mistake to confront Brianne. I'd desperately wished that I'd just gone to see the police instead. So that's where I'd headed next.

My trip to the police station had turned out equally badly. The detective that I was finally allowed to see had glanced down at a file folder in his hands, and he'd seemed distant and skeptical. To my surprise, the file had my name on it.

"I know all about your case, Ms. Farley. Brianne Walsh just called in a complaint and said that you've been harassing her. She's on her way down right now to get a restraining order against you. Maybe it'd be better if you just went on home."

"Restraining order? How could that be? I'm the victim," I sputtered. "She tried to kill me by running me off the road. My car was badly damaged. Then, someone vandalized my house and stole a bunch of my things. And now, Brianne's threatening to steal my children. I can't help but feel that she's behind everything." I was so upset that I'd burst into tears, but that had only made him look more annoyed.

"No one wants your kids, lady," he mumbled in a bored-sounding voice. "And there isn't any proof of your accusations."

12

He'd glanced down at the file, as if he were checking out something. "Your ex-husband swears that Ms. Warner was with him when both incidents happened."

"He what? You must be mistaken. He told me that she was with him during the break-in, but not when I was forced off the road." Had Michael lied to the police, just to protect Brianne? The pain of betrayal had swept through me. I'd always thought that Michael cared about my welfare. Could Brianne have intimidated him into lying to the police? And at my expense? I'd taken a deep breath.

"Michael's the one who first told me that Brianne was trying to hurt me. Maybe he's scared of her."

But none of my arguing had done one bit of good. I could see that. So, I'd finally given up and gone home. I'd cried on Mom's shoulder like I had when I was a child. Later, after I was feeling calmer, we'd talked over everything.

"Do you think it's possible that the person trying to hurt you could be someone you had trouble with at work, instead of Brianne?" Mom asked.

"Of course not. This has nothing to do with work." But, at her words, I'd gotten a funny feeling in the pit of my stomach.

"All I'm saying is that you should consider the possibility. Think back: Is there anyone you've had to reprimand at work? You're the manager of an entire department, and I know that, occasionally, you've had to correct people—sometimes even fire them. Some people really have short fuses."

"Work's not the problem!" I insisted. Then, suddenly, I'd remembered Tina Runyon, the woman I'd had to fire just before the accidents had started, because she had stolen merchandise. I'd slapped my hand over my mouth. Firing Tina had been so upsetting that I had forced the incident out of my mind.

Tina had systematically stolen merchandise over a period of about six months. The evidence of her theft was in the purchasing and sales records. When she was leaving the building with unpaid merchandise, the security guard had caught her in the act. I had been required to terminate her on the spot, and to call the police.

Could it have been Tina, and not Brianne, who was after me? The woman had seemed unhinged. I remembered being pleased when Tina hadn't been sent to jail, but had, instead, been released under a relative's supervision. But, suddenly, I wasn't happy, because Tina was free to stalk me if she wanted.

Had I falsely accused Brianne? If so, I'd done her a terrible injustice. She would have had a good reason to be furious, and to make all kinds of accusations against me. After all, Michael had been with her during the break-in.

13

After I'd gotten the kids settled into bed, I'd called the detective again. The conversation had gone badly.

"We asked you at the time if there was anyone else who might have had a grudge against you," the detective said. "You told us that there wasn't." Annoyance had sharpened his tone and I'd cringed.

I'd explained as best I could that I had forgotten about Tina, but the man's cold tone had told me that he wasn't impressed. Every word I'd uttered had only made things worse. It was almost as if I had become the little boy who'd cried "wolf" too many times.

For the next three days, I'd driven myself crazy, trying to figure out who could have wanted me dead. Saturday was my usual day off, so I was really glad when it finally rolled around. It was great to be home doing my housework, knowing that the kids were safely playing with their toys in the next room. For the first time in days, I'd started to feel safe again.

I'd glanced over at the paper bag containing two new deadbolt locks. Installing those on my doors was the next thing that I was planning to do, just in case Brianne did have a key to my house.

Suddenly, Bryan had walked into the kitchen. "Where did Jessica go?" he asked.

"I thought the two of you were playing in your room!" Panic had shot through me as he shook his head with a scared look.

Be calm, I told myself. She may be in the bathroom. But when I'd rushed to the bathroom, it was empty. Then I tore down the hall to her bedroom. My heart lurched and I thought I was going to throw up. Jessica's window was open! Someone had removed the screen, and the wind was blowing her curtains.

I'd raced into the yard, looking around desperately and screaming my daughter's name. But she was nowhere to be found. I'd dialed 911 and begged the dispatcher to send someone to help us. Then, I'd alerted Mrs. Lawsen, who'd offered to watch Bryan while I'd continued searching.

I'd called Michael on his cell phone to make sure he hadn't dropped by and picked up Jessica without telling me. He'd never done such a thing before, but I was checking every possibility. However, he'd seemed as frantic as I was when I'd told him that she was missing. He'd said that he'd be right over.

Michael had arrived shortly after the police. I was in tears, explaining what had happened, and it was a comfort to have him there. The officers had checked Jessica's bedroom and the backyard again, and were getting ready to announce an intensive citywide search when, suddenly, Jessica had wandered back into the yard. She'd seemed to appear out of nowhere.

I'd swept up my daughter into my arms and cried with joy. When the police had quizzed her, she'd clammed up, shaking her head vehemently with tears welling in her eyes. We couldn't get her to say anything. When the police asked her if she'd been hurt, she just shook her head even harder.

The police had questioned her until she was sobbing. Then, they'd finally seemed to give up. One of the officers had told me that someone from social services would be by later to interview me, and to make a report. It was evident that the officers thought that Jessica's disappearance was negligence on my part, and that knowledge had made my blood run cold. I'd had to take deep breaths to calm myself.

It's going to be okay, I reassured myself. The main thing is that the kids are okay. Everything else can be worked out. After all, I'm a responsible adult with a good job. I attend church. I can get dozens of people to vouch for me if I need to. But, in spite of all of my positive thinking, I was still scared to death. Finally, the police left.

Michael had taken me into his arms to comfort me, and the closeness had felt really good. I was tempted to ask him to stay the night, but I didn't want to give him false hope. So I'd sent him home.

The kids were so upset that I'd had to take some time and calm them down. I'd read a story from their children's Bible, and we'd sung a few songs that they had learned in Sunday School. I was about ready to let them play alone so that I could deal with the new locks, when Jessica had snuggled into my lap. She'd looked at me with her beautiful eyes and smiled.

"I don't want to live with anyone else but you, Mommy," she told me.

"Well, of course not, sweetie. This is your home."

"I don't want another mommy," she went on.

"Jessica, what on earth are you talking about?" I asked.

She'd pressed her lips tightly together. "Can't say," she mumbled. "Bad trouble if I do."

And, no argument on my part could change her mind. For a minute, I'd thought about calling the police again, but every time I'd talked to them, things had just gone from bad to worse.

So I'd decided to pack up and move in with Mom. She'd asked me to do that several times, and I'd refused. But, by that point, I was terrified enough to do anything. I was running for my life, and for my kids' lives. No way did I want to end up as another headline in the newspaper. I'd wanted to be safe, and I'd wanted to keep my kids safe.

Whoever was behind the attacks had threatened my daughter with something so frightening that she was afraid to tell me who had abducted her.

When I'd thought back, I'd remembered that Tina Runyon also

15

had a sort of fixation about children. She didn't have any of her own, and she was always saying how she'd longed to adopt a child—if only the agencies would allow her to do so. She had lamented over the shortage of children available for adoption. Was it possible that she had some kind of insane plan to steal my kids?

Brianne, of course, was the most logical person to want Jessica and Bryan, because of Michael. But if Brianne was behind all of this evil, she had to be truly insane.

I'd taken the kids upstairs with me and told them that we were going on a vacation to their grandma's, and that we had to pack. They were so excited that they'd clapped their hands and cheered.

I'd thrown their clothes into a large duffel bag while they'd packed a few toys in their backpacks. Then, we'd headed to my room, where I'd pulled a big armload of my clothes from the closet so that I could haul them downstairs to the car.

Suddenly, I'd heard the sound of glass breaking downstairs.

My heart had iced over in fear. For a moment, I couldn't move. Then, holding a trembling finger to my lips, I'd reached for my bedside phone to dial 911. The line was dead.

Pure terror had paralyzed me. What could I do? Someone was in the house, and I'd assumed that person meant to do my children or me grave harm. I'd grabbed Bryan and Jessica and led them into my large walk-in closet.

"We're going to play a game of hide and seek," I whispered to them. "No matter what happens, don't come out until I come back to get you. Do you understand?"

Bryan had looked scared, and Jessica had seemed about to cry.

"Don't be scared," I whispered. "I'll be back as soon as possible. Until then, don't make a peep."

Both of my brave children had nodded, although they were wide-eyed and scared. Young as they were, they'd understood that our lives were in jeopardy.

Then, I'd pulled some of my long skirts over their crouching bodies and covered them. "Stay hidden," I whispered again.

I'd quietly closed the closet door, then looked desperately for some kind of a weapon. If only I'd had my softball bat, but that was in the utility room. The only thing that I'd seen was a heavy paperweight that Mom had brought me from a vacation. I'd lifted it for weight.

Maybe, with my good throwing arm, I could manage one good shot with this. If I'm lucky, I thought.

I'd remembered the story of David and Goliath in the Bible as I'd slipped out of the room and quietly closed the door behind me. Please, Lord, I prayed silently, give me David's strength and good aim.

I'd peeked down the staircase, and sure enough, someone

16

dressed in black was creeping into the foyer below. The person wore a ski mask, so I couldn't tell if it was Brianne or Tina. All I knew was that, somehow, I had to save us. Then I'd seen that the person was carrying a gun. I was so terrified that I could hardly stand upright.

In that moment, I'd rejoiced that my parents had managed to pay for my pitching lessons as I was growing up. I doubted if they'd ever thought that my life might depend on that particular skill, but, in my opinion, nothing much was accidental in life. I'd always firmly believed that God planned everything.

I'd tried to remember all of the instructions that I'd ever received. Then, I'd wound up, aimed, and let the paperweight fly toward the head of the villain, using all of the strength that I'd had.

Just as I'd released the missile, the intruder had glanced up and seen me, then raised the gun. Fear had turned my legs into gelatin, but I supposed the other person was scared, too, because their finger seemed to freeze before pulling the trigger.

The paperweight had hit the intruder dead center on the temple and knocked whoever it was off balance. I'd watched the gun fly toward the front door.

I didn't know if I'd killed someone or just stunned the person, but I'd had enough sense to understand that I'd better get ahold of the gun. I'd raced downstairs as the intruder had struggled to pull up on his hands and knees.

I thanked God that I'd always been strong and fast. Fear had pumped adrenaline into my body, and I'd moved like lightning. I was down the stairs before the person had reached the gun. I'd slid across the tile toward the weapon just like the many times when I'd slid into home base, blocking the scoundrel with my shoulder and pushing their body away.

My children were upstairs, and knowing that had given me more strength and agility than I'd ever had before. My fingers had closed around the cold steel of the gun and I'd rolled over to distance myself, supporting my weight on my elbows as I'd moved. I'd pulled myself to a standing position and pointed the gun directly at the attacker.

"One move and you're dead!" I shouted. I'd meant every word.

The person had frozen.

I'd stood there with the gun aimed at the monster who had turned my happy life into a nightmare. For a moment, I'd seriously thought about pulling the trigger. The police had given me no reason to trust their protection. I was pretty certain at that point that the intruder was Brianne. But what if she told the police that it was all some kind of mistake, and the authorities believed her, instead of me? My life would continue being the nightmare that it had been.

I knew that the state I lived in had a "Make my day" law. If you killed an intruder inside your house, then it was considered self-defense. I didn't know much about guns, but as close as I'd stood to that person, I knew that I wouldn't miss. I'd lifted the gun and aimed.

The person had cringed and stepped backward. I'd tried to will myself to pull the trigger, but I just couldn't. Somehow, the frightened body language of the cowering human being before me had spoken to my heart, and I couldn't shoot.

But how was I going to summon the police? My telephone wires had been cut, and my cell phone was in my purse in the living room.

Then, I'd heard a scuffling sound and realized the kids were on the stairs behind me.

As calmly as I could, I'd asked Bryan to slip around me and get the cell phone out of my handbag in the living room. Then, I'd spoken harshly to the intruder.

"If you move, whoever you are, it'll be the last thing that you ever do," I said coldly. And I'd meant it.

Bryan, brave little boy that he was, did exactly as I'd asked him. But he'd surprised me because I could hear him in the living room, dialing 911 himself and telling the operator that his mommy had a bad guy on the floor and needed help. I had painstakingly drilled both kids on memorizing our address, and I'd heard him give it perfectly. I didn't think I'd ever been prouder in my life.

"Stay in the living room, Bryan!" I shouted.

"Okay, Mommy," he called back, every inch the little man. Jessica had pressed closely against the back of my legs.

I'd held the gun on the intruder until the police had arrived. I'd so wanted to pull the mask from that face and to confront Brianne, but I was afraid that she might manage to overpower me and gain control of the gun. I couldn't take that chance.

I'd heard sirens, then a pounding on the front door. I'd slipped around the prone figure and opened the door to let them in. Then I'd stepped back and pulled off the ski mask. When I saw who was lying on the floor, I'd almost collapsed.

It wasn't Brianne. It wasn't even a woman at all!

Michael, my almost ex-husband, had gazed up at me with a wild, trapped look on his face.

"Michael!" I exclaimed.

"I just wanted you back, Janine," he whispered. "I love you. I thought that, if you got scared enough, you'd need me. But you didn't, so I had to keep doing worse and worse things. Your determination to be independent was ruining my dream of having a wife and children."

"You forced me off the road," I said incredulously. "You could have killed me. Did you come back to finish the job?"

"No, of course not. When I borrowed my mom's old car, I only

18

meant to get your attention. Then I was going to drop back and let you escape, after you were good and scared. But that man showed up and I panicked. All I intended to do today was to scare you."

But the police officer had checked his gun, and it was loaded with real bullets. After the officers had asked their questions, they'd hauled him toward their squad car.

"I'll never stop loving you, Janine!" Michael called out.

The kids and I had clung to each other.

"I don't want to live with Michael," Jessica told me. "I don't like him anymore. He said if I told you he'd taken me away this afternoon, that he'd hurt you. That scared me. I didn't tell, but I really don't like him anymore."

"Don't worry, sweetie. You aren't living with anyone but me and Bryan." I was shaking so badly that my teeth rattled. I'd looked desperately at the detective who had just shown up. He was the same one I'd talked to at the station a short while before. Only now, he was looking at me with a lot of sympathy.

"How long will he be in jail?" I asked. I'd almost shot my ex-husband, and I'd honestly wondered if it wouldn't have been better if I had. "Will my kids and I be safe when Michael gets out?"

"Hard to say." He'd shrugged. "If the courts decide that he's crazy, they'll send him to a hospital until he's stabilized, then, perhaps, release him. Off the record, it might have been better if you'd pulled that trigger."

I'd taken a long breath and fought the panic that had threatened to overpower me. Then, I'd lifted my head high.

"No. I did the only thing that I could do," I said. "And because of that, I believe that God will protect me."

He'd shrugged again. "You've got guts, lady. I'll say that for you."

That was five months ago. Michael was evaluated by the state and then hospitalized. At the present time, he's being treated by the state for his mental illness, but I don't know how long he'll be there.

Maybe I would have been safer if I'd killed him when I had the chance, but that would have been a very wrong thing to do. The man is sick. He needs help. And it's illegal to take the law into your own hands. Besides, I'm trusting God to protect me from danger. He has helped me before, and I believe that He will keep on taking care of my kids and me.

Even so, sometimes I have trouble sleeping at night.

THE END

DID PASSION MAKE
MY LOVER A KILLER?
His wife is dead

Roger and Anna had almost finished eating breakfast when got I downstairs that morning. The kitchen radio was on for the morning news broadcast.

"Hi, sleepyhead," Anna said. "I put your orange juice back in the refrigerator." She dropped a slice of bread into the toaster and poured my coffee while I went to the refrigerator for my juice. Suddenly, my fingers froze on the door handle.

"Police are investigating last night's murder of Mrs. Janice Wyndham, whose husband called police after finding the victim's body in their Ridgefield home," an announcer said. "Hugh Wyndham, an executive at a local firm, has been taken into custody for further questioning. Police were unable to find any evidence to support the husband's theory of a prowler. The couple's only child, Steven, is away at boarding school in another state."

Clinging to the refrigerator door for support, I heard my brother's voice, which was by the sudden tumult in my mind.

"So, there was something wrong!" he exclaimed. "I suspected it, when that kid ran away last spring. But, who'd have ever thought that the guy would be capable of murder?"

I managed to get the refrigerator door shut, but I stumbled as I fled past Roger and Anna toward the hall.

"Hey, sis! What's—" I heard Roger call after me. Then, Anna's gentle voice cut him off.

Somehow, I got up to my room. I locked the door and then fell across my bed, my body shaking as though it had been chilled.

I heard Roger knocking on my door. "Come on, let me in," he said.

I sat up and pushed my hair back with both hands. Pull yourself together! I told myself sharply. It isn't really your fault. You didn't know what would happen.

I stood up, went to the door, and unlocked it. Roger threw it open and stood in the doorway, his eyes probing mine sharply.

"It was that news bulletin, wasn't it?" he demanded.

"That what?" I repeated.

"The bulletin that we just heard on the radio," he said.

Deny it, I thought. Deny everything!

I put my trembling fingers against my temples. "I'm sorry—I

didn't hear it. I woke up with a bad headache and I—I thought I was going to be sick," I told him. Somehow, I managed to fashion my lips into a feeble smile. "I'm sorry if I scared you."

He let out his breath slowly. "Oh. Well, that boy, Steven's, mother was murdered last night. They're holding Hugh Wyndham."

"Oh, Roger!" I exclaimed in a shocked voice. "That poor little boy!" It was magnificent acting. I turned to the mirror. "Tell Anna that I'll be right down."

My brother hesitated for a moment, then went on down the stairs.

When I got downstairs again, Anna didn't look at me. She just poured fresh coffee for me and put my orange juice beside my plate.

"Isn't that awful, about the Wyndhams?" I asked. "Roger told me that they're holding Hugh for questioning."

"Yes," Anna murmured. "Of course, they're still investigating his story of a prowler, too. He claims that he didn't get home until midnight."

Roger was pulling on his jacket in the hall. "It's a pretty flimsy story," he commented. "They'll never buy it. They'll be questioning all of us." He looked pointedly at me. "You'd better watch your step. They'll be looking for the 'other woman,' you know."

A shiver ran through me, but I managed to nod. "I suppose so," I agreed.

"It's funny," Anna mused, following Roger to the front door for their good-bye kiss. "You never believe that these kinds of things will happen so close to home."

I gulped down my coffee and got into the hall before Anna could come back and begin questioning me. It was hard to lie to my intelligent sister-in-law.

"It's sort of windy," Anna told me. "You'd better take a jacket."

I found one in the hall closet and put it on. I heard Roger's car as it headed down the lane. A few years earlier, Roger and Anna had bought a huge piece of property and had remodeled the old farmhouse where they lived. We'd all been proud of the result.

The money that I paid my brother and his wife every month for room and board helped to cover their mortgage payment, and Anna joked about always having a baby-sitter available. It had never been any chore for me to watch my adorable nephew, Bryan, who was eighteen months old, while Anna and Roger went out for their weekly "date."

"Be careful, honey," Anna told me. "Don't let anyone intimidate you."

But, as I drove downtown, panic was already a blinding, dizzying current that was rushing through me. The turbulent emotions of the past few months seemed to be surging through my mind. I knew I had to sort out my emotions and clear my head for the ordeal I had yet to face. Yet, even as I tried to think back to the beginning, an undercurrent of horror kept racing through my heart.

Oh, Hugh, I never meant for you to do something so terrible! I thought.

My most vivid memory was of that moment, the night before, when Hugh had been holding me fiercely, and his voice had been grim.

"I've got to figure out some way," he'd told me. "And I will, Kirsten! Do you hear me? I will!"

But, oh, not this way, Hugh! I thought. How could you have thought that murder would solve anything? Or, had murder grown out of a final, terrible argument between them?

The announcer had said that the murder had been committed at around midnight. But, it had only been eleven when Hugh had left me. What had happened in that hour?

I hadn't known about Janice Wyndham a year earlier when Hugh had come from Chicago to work for Casey Worthington, my boss. Hugh had stayed at a hotel and had eaten all of his meals in restaurants. That had been my first concern about the new man in our company. I'd felt sorry that he'd been eating nothing but restaurant food. And so, I'd invited him to dinner at our house.

Anna and Roger had been their usual, friendly selves, and it had been fun watching Hugh Wyndham relax in the warm atmosphere. He'd adored Bryan, who'd only been a few months old at the time.

He'd come over for dinner one more time before I'd found out about his wife and small son, and by that time, I had fallen hopelessly in love.

It had been on the night of his second visit that he'd told me. He'd had car trouble that morning and had to bring his car in to be serviced, so I'd offered him a ride home to my house.

"Why not just ride out with me and one of us will bring you back to the hotel later?" I'd suggested.

We'd never really been alone together before that night, and as I handed him my keys in the parking lot, a quiver of anticipation had run through me. There'd been a strange, electric undercurrent—a sense of eager recognition that had existed between us almost from the first. There'd been the swift blaze of awareness in Hugh's eyes the time our hands had accidentally touched. But, finally—that night, perhaps—I'd hoped that we could capture that elusive something.

He drove expertly, but as we'd turned off onto the country road from which our lane led, he'd slowed the car and looked at me.

"Kirsten, before we get there, are you sure that you'll be able to drive me home?" he asked. "You aren't afraid to drive back alone afterward, are you?"

"No," I assured him, my heart pounding with happiness. "Don't watch me blush, Hugh. To be honest, I'd hoped that you'd suggest my driving you back to your car later."

He'd stepped on the gas again. He wasn't smiling.

And then, we were on our lane and Roger was coming toward us from the little barn that was almost as important to him as the house.

"Hi, Hugh," Roger called. "Want to see my barn while Anna and Kirsten get dinner on the table?"

Hugh had gone off with Roger then, and I'd gone into the house to help Anna.

"You like him, don't you, sweetie?" Anna asked as she stirred flour into the skillet for gravy.

"Sure," I admitted. "Don't you?"

"Very much. Only—well, it seems a bit odd that a man like that—one who's so attractive and all, hasn't ever been married. Or, has he? Do you know?"

I gave her a secret smile. "No, but I'm sure I'll know everything about him after tonight. He asked me if I'd drive him back, so I guess he wants to talk to me." I squeezed her arm. "Keep your fingers crossed."

"You know I will, Kirsten," she told me. "That's what I want for you so much—a man as fine as Roger, a home, and kids—"

"Kids, she says," Roger said from the back door. "The woman's talking plural at last. Hugh, after I'd almost given up—"

"Roger!" Anna chided, laughing. "Hello, Hugh. I hope the smell of that barn won't ruin your dinner." She gave him her hand, smiling. "Take him into the living room, Kirsten."

"Couldn't I just stay in a corner here, out of your way, where I can smell this heavenly aroma?" he asked.

Roger answered for her. "Sure. I think the kitchen is the nicest room in the house. Anna is a good cook, Hugh. I keep telling Kirsten to learn all she can from her."

"Shame on you, Roger," Anna protested. "Kirsten did a very good job of cooking your meals right up until you went into the service." She pulled a pan of golden biscuits from the oven. "That wasn't easy for a girl who was still in high school—with all the household chores to do, too."

"Stop," I told her, my face burning. "Hugh doesn't care about our personal history."

"But, I do care—very much," he insisted. "It's very interesting."

His eyes were on me and there was such warmth in them that I had to swallow before I could speak again. "Here—since you want to help, put this platter on the table in there, will you?" I asked him.

Dinner was pleasant, with Roger and Anna full of easy chatter and Bryan beating his spoon on his high chair tray to get his share of attention. When dinner was over and the men had moved into the dining room, Roger put his hand on Hugh's shoulder.

"There's nothing like a home, a good wife, and children to make life good," he told him.

"You're right," I heard Hugh say soberly.

As we rinsed the dishes, I turned to Anna. "I hope Hugh doesn't get the idea that Roger's trying to marry me off."

"Oh, don't worry. I'm sure that Roger's probably talking politics by now," Anna said reassuringly.

At nine, after a comfortable few hours of conversation, Hugh stood up to go.

"I'll drive you back," I said quickly, and Roger just grinned.

Hugh did the driving. He stopped the car just before we turned off the county road. He sat there quietly for a while, and I sensed that he was groping for words. But, at last, he turned to me.

"Before I say anything, Kirsten—" he began. Then, he reached for me, drew my willing body close, and held me pressed warmly against him for a long time. I could feel the strong beat of his heart, and his breathing grew ragged. He put one hand under my chin and lifted my face close to his.

"Oh, Kirsten," he whispered, and then, his mouth was on mine. The gentleness was gone then, and the flame in him lit fire in my own blood as my lips parted in response under his.

He broke away at last and buried his face against my throat. "Oh, Kirsten, why did I ever come to this town?" he groaned.

Stunned, I pulled back, straining to see his face in the dark.

He shook his head as though to clear away the confusion of his emotions. "I had no right to kiss you, Kirsten," he said brokenly.

"Why?" I whispered.

"I have a wife—a wife and a son, who's almost eight years old."

I felt as though all the blood in my body were draining away, and suddenly, my teeth were chattering.

"I shouldn't have gone to your brother's home," Hugh went on in a tired voice. "It was bad enough before—all the little things at the office, your hand touching mine, seeing you every day—"

I swallowed, but the painful lump in my throat didn't go away. When I finally could speak, my voice sounded unnatural and strained.

"I invited you there as a friend," I told him. "It's all right. There's no reason for you to feel guilty. You never said anything to make me think that there was anything more between us."

"No, I was very virtuous, wasn't I?" he asked fiercely. "I didn't say anything—but I should have. I knew that I should tell you about Janice and my son, but—" He paused, and I could see the stricken, lost look in his eyes.

24

"There's a little justification, Kirsten," he went on finally. "I really believed that it was over between Janice and me. She was furious when I sold my business, but I just couldn't go on living my life her way—always determined to keep up appearances, no matter how much it was killing me. I have never been emotionally equipped for that sort of competition—that strain. But, Janice had to hold on to the social rung that she'd clawed her way up to." He gave a short laugh. "Up to? Actually, I'd call it a downward climb. It was a life that consisted of drinking, dirty stories, being expected to paw other men's wives any time you found yourself in a corner with them. Janice thought it was wonderful. Well, I hated every part of it, so I quit." He sat there silently for a moment.

"I sold out. She said if I left Chicago, I'd go alone. So, when Casey Worthington made me an offer, I took it—alone. But, there's Steven, my son. I've worried myself sick about leaving him. And now—well, for some reason, Janice has decided to come here."

My teeth were closed so tightly on the flesh of one wrist that I could taste blood. Don't you dare cry! I thought. Don't be more of a fool than you've already been. Thinking that you could have a man like Hugh—what a fool!

"For Steven's sake, I have to let her come. He needs me." His voice was pleading. "You can see that, can't you, Kirsten?"

I nodded. I couldn't speak—my throat was thick with unshed tears.

Hugh sat with his hands gripped tightly on the wheel. "I've hurt you," he said, "and I'm sorry. But, remember this one thing—I wasn't toying with you. I honestly thought that my marriage was over and except for Steven—" He turned his face toward me, but he kept his hands on the wheel. "I love you, Kirsten. I don't know what I can do about it but, for what it's worth to your pride, I love you more than I ever knew I could love any woman."

He started the car. "That's what had to be said, Kirsten."

We rode the rest of the way in silence. When we pulled up in front of the hotel, Hugh put his hand on mine.

"Forgive me, Kirsten," he begged, and then he got out and strode into the hotel. My eyes were flooded with tears as I moved behind the wheel. I sat there until I could control them, then drove slowly home—too numb for thought.

When I got there, Roger had gone to bed, but Anna was in the living room, mending. She gave me a quick look, then went on with her work. I dropped limply into a chair, leaned back, and shut my eyes.

"Something wrong?" she asked gently.

"Yes, there's something wrong," I answered. "He's married."

25

"Well, honey," Anna told me, "if he'd been the right one for you, there wouldn't be any wife. I'm sorry, but you'll get over it."

"Sure," I agreed. "Sure, I'll get over it." I got up, hugged Anna, and went up to bed.

Hugh's wife and son moved to town the next week. Hugh found an almost-new house for them in the area's newest subdivision, and the furniture arrived the day before Janice Wyndham did.

Mr. Worthington had been home all week with a cold, but on Thursday, he asked me to come into his office for a meeting. That's why Eunice Dwyer, the bookkeeper, was the only one in the office when Mrs. Wyndham stopped by, looking for Hugh, who was out on an appointment.

"Boy, is she ever a snob!" Eunice exclaimed. "She's one of those women who smiles with her mouth and keeps the help in their place with her eyes."

I didn't answer, and after a moment, Eunice looked at me curiously. "It was kind of a blow to find out that there was a Mrs. Wyndham, wasn't it?"

"Was it?" I countered coldly. "Did you have designs on him?"

Eunice laughed. "Not me—you. Don't try to lie to me. I've seen the look in your eyes—and his."

I looked down at my desk. Eunice had never missed a chance for a dig at me, not since the time I'd gone on a double date with her and two men that I'd never met. We'd gone to the movies and out to dinner, and then, we'd gone for a ride. After two hours of sparring with my half-drunk date, I'd asked to be let out of the car. Then, I'd called for a taxi and gone home. Eunice had never forgiven me for leaving her there, and there'd been no love lost between us ever since.

During those next months, through the Christmas season and into the spring, I lived in a strange sort of shell. Life on the surface seemed routine, but underneath was a surging, never-diminishing hunger. The sight of Hugh, each time he came into the office, grazed the raw wound of my heart. He tried never to meet my eyes, and he stayed as far away from me as possible. But I could feel him there. It was as though there'd been an invisible but unbreakable bond woven between us.

I'd thought about quitting my job, and moving to some other town to live and work. But, while I knew that Roger and Anna could manage without my money every month, I also knew that they'd have more of a struggle. Besides, with no other relatives in the world, I'd had enough loneliness for a lifetime during the years when my brother had been in the service.

And so, I stayed. Each morning, I told myself that it would be easier. Today, I'd think, he'll be just another man. But, when he'd come in to check his mail, he was never just another man. He was Hugh, and the pain in my heart would still be there.

Bryan's birthday was on a Saturday in the spring. Anna had planned a picnic in the park, where Bryan could also see the animals in a small zoo. We were all standing by the children's zoo entrance when some friends of theirs came by and asked Roger and Anna to come and see their new car. They left Bryan with me, and they hadn't been gone for five minutes when a hand touched my arm. I turned to look into Hugh's face. My heart gave a dizzying leap.

"Steven," Hugh said, and an adorable little boy looked up. "This is my son, Kirsten. Steven, Kirsten works with Daddy. And this is her little nephew, Bryan. Hi, Bryan."

"Hi," Bryan said, reaching for Steven's bag of cotton candy.

"I'm going to feed the ducks," Steven told him gravely. "Do you want to help, Bryan?"

"Yes!" Bryan said happily. Steven bent down to the smaller boy, holding his hand with such gentleness that I turned around to exchange smiles with Hugh. But, there was no smile on his face. Instead, there was such an agony of despair that a little cry escaped me.

"Oh, don't, Hugh. Please!" I told him.

His face stiffened. "Sorry," he mumbled. "I stood back there watching you, and I guess I just couldn't help it. You looked almost happy then, Kirsten. I shouldn't have spoiled it."

"I am happy," I said sharply. "How could you spoil it?" Then as his anguished eyes met mine again, I knew that I had to be honest. "That was a lie, Hugh. I wish it wasn't. I wish I could be happy, but—"

The children had walked over to the small pond and were throwing bread to the ducks.

"Kirsten, I can't stand it," he whispered.

"You have a wife," I reminded him, trying to keep my voice steady.

"What a farce that is!" He laughed bitterly. "I've begged her to divorce me. She says that she'll do it when she's ready—not before. She just laughs when I tell her that all I want is to keep Steven. She pampers the boy—likes to show him off. But, if her mood changes, she shuts him away from her. The poor kid is getting so that he's afraid to trust her. I don't know—it's such an intangible thing, Kirsten. No court would ever understand."

I didn't answer. I kept my eyes on the boys. Hugh's son was so like him—a beautiful child with kind eyes, and the same vulnerable sweetness in his smile.

"He's a nice boy," Hugh said, as though seeking my approval.

"He's like you," I told him gently.

27

"I hope he'll grow up with better judgment," Hugh answered fiercely.

"There are some people coming," I said. Then, we walked over to where the children were eating the cotton candy and saw that the bread was gone.

"They finished all the bread, Daddy," Steven said earnestly.

"That's okay, son. Anyway, we've got to go. We haven't seen the penguins yet."

"Daddy, has Bryan got a cow? He keeps saying 'cow.'"

I answered him, smiling. "Yes, we have a cow and some chickens at our farm, Steven. Have you ever milked a cow?"

He shook his head, his eyes bright. "I wish I could see the cow."

"Well," I said, "maybe you can, someday—"

"Couldn't you come with us and see the penguins—please?" Steven begged.

Tears stung my eyelids. The child was lonely.

"We've seen the penguins, sweetie, and Bryan's parents will be back soon," I told him gently. "We have to wait here for them."

The next day, in the office, Hugh walked over to my desk. "Do you think your brother and his wife would mind if Steven came out to see the cow after dinner tonight? He's talked of nothing else since yesterday."

"I'm sure it would be fine, Hugh," I told him.

Excitement beat crazily in my heart for the rest of the day. I knew in my head that I was heading toward the edge of a precipice, but my heart didn't care.

It was seven-thirty that evening when Hugh arrived. Roger had delayed milking for Steven's benefit, so I let him do the honors at the barn. I forced myself to stay inside, and an hour later, they came in. Hugh was carrying the milk pail and Roger was carrying Bryan. Steven's eyes were bright with excitement.

"Mr. Lerner showed me how to milk!" he said. "And, how to bed Daisy down with hay, and—"

Hugh grinned, his eyes avoiding mine. "Maybe I'm raising a farmer," he said.

"A man could do worse," Roger answered. "A farmer has problems, but the rewards can be great."

All too soon, they were saying good night. Hugh's eyes met mine for one long look but we didn't even touch hands. I went to bed with a forlorn yearning inside of me.

It was a few weeks later when we learned that Steven was missing. Bryan was in bed, and Anna and I had been finishing the dishes, when Roger called to us from the living room.

"Hey, Anna, Kirsten—listen to this!" he called.

28

Anna went in, but I waited to hang up the dish towels and turn off the kitchen lights before I followed her. Roger had turned up the volume on the television and was standing there, watching the news intently.

"Area volunteers have been organized and will leave immediately for a search of the surrounding area. Authorities are inclined to discount the theory of kidnapping until a search has been made. Residents of the area are asked to help search for eight-year-old Steven Wyndham. We repeat—" The announcer's voice was drowned out by the cry of anguish that I couldn't suppress.

"When?" I finally managed to whisper.

"He left school at the normal time," Roger explained. "The crossing guard saw him headed toward his house, but, apparently, he never got there." Roger strode to the closet for his jacket. "I'm going to help look for him," he announced, then turned back to kiss Anna. I saw him pull her close for a moment. "A few years from now, that might be Bryan," he said.

Anna stood in the porch watching Roger drive away, then she came back in and locked the door.

"Maybe he just decided to run away. Lots of kids do that, at some point," I suggested, but my voice was shaking. How Hugh must be suffering! I thought.

"At eight years old?" Anna protested. "Poor Mrs. Wyndham! If Bryan ever—well, I think I'd lose my mind," she said grimly.

The regular news broadcast was on by then but, after a while, they cut in with another bulletin. It seemed that the highway patrol had joined the search. The newscaster said that the police were now considering the possibility of abduction by a stranger.

A low rumble outside made us glance at each other in dismay. It was thunder. Before we could get to the window, we heard the sharp blast of rain against the pane.

"Oh, Kirsten!" Anna cried. "That poor child's out there in this horrible weather!"

I snapped off the lights and looked over Anna's shoulder. We could hardly see beyond the window at first, but, as another flash of lightning illuminated the yard, I felt Anna shiver. I put my arm around her, knowing that she was thinking of Bryan, and seeing him as an eight-year-old boy who was lost.

"They'll find him," I assured her. "Kids do crazy things. They sometimes get the idea that they aren't wanted or something—"

Anna turned away from the window and snapped on the lights again. "I wish Roger had taken his raincoat," she murmured.

The episode of thunder was brief, but at ten o'clock, there was another storm. The thunder and lightning had grown sharper and the wind had risen. Suddenly, a lightning bolt struck somewhere close. Anna gave a stifled cry as we heard a splintering, then the crashing of a tree in the yard.

The silence that followed was almost more frightening. Anna rushed for the stairs and I could hear Bryan whimper, and then, the sound of her soothing lullaby.

Then, I heard the other crying—from outside the house. I yanked a coat from the closet and threw it around me.

"I'm going out to see what that noise is," I called up to her. I opened the door just as another streak of lightning illuminated the yard.

He was climbing out from under a branch of the fallen tree—a little boy with hair plastered flat and torn clothes.

"It's all right, Steven," I called to him. "You're all right now." But, when I lifted him, he gave a little moan. I carried him across the lawn to the house. Anna already had the door open.

"Call the police station," I told her. "Hugh's probably there."

I pulled off Steven's wet clothing as gently as possible. His eyelids flickered and he winced. When I removed his sock, I saw a gash on his leg.

I could hear Anna on the telephone in the hall, but Steven was talking now, too—talking between chills that shook his little body.

"Don't tell them," he begged. "Please, Miss Lerner! I was all right in the barn until—well, the lightning scared me, sort of, and I thought if I could get closer to the house just until it stopped—"

In Roger's barn! That was where Steven had sought refuge.

Anna came in with gauze and adhesive tape. She knelt down beside Steven, examined his leg, and got right to work.

"Hugh was there," she reported. "He'll be right over with a doctor."

Steven turned his face away from us, but not before I'd seen the despair in his eyes. He didn't want to see his father.

It wasn't more than ten minutes before the cars turned in the lane. The news was still on, announcing that the missing child had been found—quieting the fears of the community. Anna turned it off and went to let Hugh, the doctor, and two policemen in.

Hugh came across the room, pulling off his jacket as he walked. He had eyes for no one but Steven.

"Hello, son," he said quietly, kneeling down beside the couch.

Steven didn't turn his face from the wall. I saw Hugh lean closer and touch the boy's face. "You've had a rough night, haven't you?" he asked gently. "But, everything's all right now."

Suddenly, Steven was in his father's arms, his body pressed tight against him, his arms straining around Hugh's neck.

"Daddy—Daddy!" he sobbed. "I didn't want you to know—"

"It's okay now, son," Hugh interrupted. "Let's have the doctor check you over and see if there's any damage."

"I'm okay," Steven said, trying to control his sobs. But, he let the doctor examine him.

Upstairs, Bryan whimpered again, and Anna went up to him. I slipped out to the kitchen and made some coffee. I'd made some sandwiches, too, when I heard Roger come in the front door.

"That coffee smells good," Hugh said from the kitchen doorway. "Steven fell asleep. Exhausted, I guess. I want to thank all of you."

I disconnected the coffeepot before turning to face him. "Why would a child do a crazy thing like that?" I asked wonderingly.

Hugh's eyes met mine, and a flush rose in his cheeks. "It's usually because of insecurity, don't you think? So, apparently, my way of handling our problem hasn't solved it."

I put a heaping tray of food into his hands. "Sandwiches," I said lamely. Then, I looked at him seriously. "I'm no psychologist. You've got Steven back. Why worry about abstract problems now?"

"Abstract? Look, Kirsten, before he went to sleep, Steven was begging me not to take him home. He said that maybe, he could work here for his meals, and maybe, you could fix a place in the barn for him to sleep. He said I could come and see him every day." Hugh's face looked grim. "He won't explain why he's so upset. He insists that he won't tell anyone why—even if they send him to jail."

I could only stare at him, too shocked to speak.

"I don't know what to do," he went on. He shrugged helplessly. "Forgive me, Kirsten. You've had enough trouble with Steven and me."

"Don't even think that," I admonished. "Don't be a fool, Hugh!" I picked up the coffeepot and pushed past him into the living room.

Anna was sitting in a chair beside the couch where Steven slept. Roger and the doctor were deep in conversation.

"Hot coffee will hit the spot," the doctor said, and took a cup.

The men drank their coffee and ate all of the sandwiches. Then the doctor stood up, stretching. "Well, you'd better get that boy home. His mother must be going crazy with worry."

"Yes." Hugh pulled himself up. There was a weariness in his posture. He picked up Steven. The boy stirred and settled again. For an instant, Hugh stood there, looking down into his son's face, and in his own was an agony of love and concern.

No one spoke as Roger opened the door for them. Perhaps they all sensed the strain in Hugh, or maybe they'd heard Steven's pleading earlier.

Hugh paused on the porch. "I can't thank you enough—"

"Forget it," Roger said. "We're just glad that Steven's safe."

31

I stood in the doorway until I couldn't hear the sound of Hugh's car anymore, then I went back to Anna and Roger.

"Why on earth would a child get himself into such a panic about going home?" Anna asked.

"Who knows what goes on in a child's mind?" Roger asked, yawning. "How about coming to bed? I'm exhausted."

But, Anna couldn't drop the subject. "He wasn't running away from his father—that much was evident. That woman must be a strange one," she mused.

"You go to bed, Anna," I told her. "I'll clean up."

The boss called to Hugh when he came into the office the next morning. "How's the boy, Hugh?" he asked. "Is he still upset?"

"No, he's all right. His throat's a bit sore—that's all," Hugh answered.

"What on earth made him pick Kirsten's barn?" Eunice asked curiously.

"He likes cows," Hugh answered, and turned away.

The weeks that followed fell into a slow, deadly routine, charged only by my electric awareness of Hugh's presence in the office each day. He was carefully polite to Eunice and me, but occasionally, I'd meet his eyes and they'd fill with such obvious pain that my own yearning sprang to vivid life again. It seemed impossible that Eunice and Mr. Worthington didn't feel the tension, but if they did, neither had ever mentioned it.

That fall, Hugh enrolled Steven in a boarding school in another town. On the morning after Hugh's return, I heard Mr. Worthington speaking to him.

"That boy's awfully young to be separated from everything that's familiar to him, Hugh. Are you sure that sending him to boarding school was the right thing to do?"

"Yes," Hugh told him. "You must know that I don't like the idea of having him so far from me, don't you? But, this is better than having him running away again."

It was a few weeks later that the dynamite on which I'd been sitting exploded. I'd worked late on a special project. I'd called Anna to tell her not to save any dinner for me. I'd told her that I'd have something sent in.

It was dark when I started home. Just before turning onto the road to my house, I saw a car parked there. I didn't recognize it as Hugh's until he leaned out and called to me. I stepped on the brake.

"Kirsten, I've been waiting for you," he said.

I hesitated, my heart beating rapidly, my mind conflicted. Then, on a reckless impulse, I nodded and drove for a few blocks. Hugh pulled up behind me and came up to my car. I moved over and he got in behind the wheel. He started the car without a word, and turned off on the road that led toward the lake.

"This was a dirty trick, I know," he apologized, "but I had to talk to you."

He pulled off the road near the lake's edge and we got out.

"It should be beautiful on the lake," he murmured. "The moon will be over the trees in a few minutes."

As though in a dream, I put my hand in his and we walked along the path that headed down to the lake. I remembered that when we'd been in high school, the kids had come to the lake to be alone.

Maybe they still do, I thought uneasily, then remembered with relief that there was a football game being held at the high school that night.

We found a spot where fallen leaves made a thin cover for the grass. Hugh took off his coat, spread it out, and we sat down. The lake was as smooth and shining as a silver ribbon in the light of the rising moon.

For a long minute, we sat very still. Then, suddenly, I was in his arms and his face was against mine.

"Oh, Kirsten—Kirsten," he whispered. Then, everything was shut out except for the wonderful warmth of his arms—of his mouth finding mine. . . .

After a while, we lay quietly with the moonlight in our eyes. The stars hung so low that it seemed we might almost reach up and touch them. We talked for a long time, and it was pleasant talk, of little things—music we both loved, memories we'd never shared with anyone before, dreams that had suddenly become vital and real.

But, at last, the wind rose and the night had begun to get chilly. I shivered, and Hugh put his arm around me again. I shook my head and moved away.

"It's been like a dream tonight," I murmured. "Only—it isn't a dream. Tomorrow we'll wake up and we'll be starving to be together again. But, we mustn't be, Hugh—ever again."

He sighed. "You're right, of course, Kirsten, but—"

I got to my feet. Hugh picked up his coat and shook the leaves from it.

"There isn't any 'but,' Hugh," I reminded him. "Not as long as you have a wife."

We heard it then—the sharp snapping of a twig, and the whispers. Then, suddenly, a flashlight blazed in our faces. With one swift sweep of his arm, Hugh pushed me behind him. The light went off, there was laughter and the scramble of feet, and then, the intruders dashed off into the trees beyond the path.

"Hugh," I whispered, stunned and shaking.

He held me with a tense arm, leading me back toward the car.

"Kirsten, I'm sorry." His voice was troubled. "It was just kids, I suppose—snooping around. They probably don't know us."

"But, what if they did?" It hadn't been as incriminating as it had looked, but who would have believed that?

We got in the car and Hugh headed toward town.

"I hate them for spoiling it," he told me quietly.

"They aren't to blame," I insisted. "It's our own fault."

We pulled up behind Hugh's car, but for a moment he sat there, brooding. The fierceness of his voice when he spoke again had startled me.

"I wish you'd marry some nice guy, Kirsten, and let me out of this—this hell!"

Anger blazed through me. "And drag one more person into it?"

He put a hand over his eyes. "Oh, I know. But, I love you so much. I don't see how I can go on without you."

"You'll go on," I told him firmly. "You'll go on as long as you don't have the—the guts to do anything about it."

Instantly, I was horrified at having said what I had. The fact was, I had never consciously even thought such a thing before. How could I have said such a thing? I heard Hugh's gasp and I turned quickly. In the dim light, I could see the shocked bewilderment in his eyes.

"I didn't mean that, Hugh. I don't know why I—" I stammered.

"But, you're right," he told me sadly. "That's what's wrong. I lack the guts to change my situation."

"Hugh, please! I didn't mean it the way it sounded. It's just—I can't think of anything else. I can't date anyone else. I've thought of going away, but I can't even make myself do that. I'm the one who's got no courage."

He sat very still, his hands clenched on the wheel. But, finally, he pulled me against him once more. The roughness of his hands and voice frightened me.

"I'm the one who's got to work it out," he told me. "We can't go on this way. We both know that. I've got to figure some way—and I will, Kirsten. Do you hear me? I will!"

I let him go then, without a word. I drove home slowly. As I got out of my car, I glanced at my watch. It was just eleven o'clock. I was relieved to see that only the hall light was on in the house. I let myself in and slipped quietly up to bed, glad that Roger and Anna hadn't stayed awake worrying about me.

For a long time, I lay there in the dark, trying to think. Who were the kids who had spied on us? How long had they been there, listening? What had we been talking about, just before they'd confronted us?

But, somehow, the memory was blurred and at last, exhausted by my emotions, I fell so sound asleep that I didn't even hear my alarm in the morning. I went downstairs, already running late. And that was when the news of Janice Wyndham's murder had exploded in my face. . . .

When I got to the office, Eunice and two other women were in a huddle. Eunice's face was alive with excitement.

"Have you heard about Hugh's wife? Right under our noses—a murder!" she exclaimed.

"You needn't look so pleased about it," one of the women protested. "It might have happened to any one of us."

Eunice's laugh was scornful. "You don't believe all that nonsense about a prowler," she scoffed.

Just then, Mr. Worthington came in and Eunice headed immediately for her desk. I was already waiting for the meeting with Mr. Worthington that I normally had every morning. He stopped to speak to some of the employees, who nodded in sober agreement. Then, he came on through the office, nodding to Eunice and me. His face was grave.

According to routine, he buzzed me and I went in to his office. "This business with Hugh Wyndham is bad, Kirsten," he said immediately.

"Awful," I murmured, keeping my eyes down.

"Hugh Wyndham couldn't murder anyone. I'd bet my last dollar on that. I knew that boy when he was working his way through high school—helping to support his mother."

I stared at him. He believed Hugh's story. He believed in Hugh! A flicker of hope stirred in me, then died. Mr. Worthington didn't know about me—about the night before, about my cruel taunt, or, about Hugh's desperation. . . .

"I talked with Hugh this morning," he continued. "I've retained Donald Emmons to represent him. And, I must warn you, Kirsten— unless they find that prowler quickly, they'll question us. All of us."

What had Roger said? He'd told me that they'd be looking for the "other woman."

I went out to my desk and began working on my computer, but my fingers were so stiff that I made countless mistakes. Mr. Worthington called Eunice, and when she came out of his office, she looked unhappy.

"In my book, it's still nonsense," she muttered as she passed my desk.

Somehow, I got through the morning. I was exhausted, though, from worrying about Hugh, and about Steven. When I came back from lunch at two, two men were waiting near my desk. I caught a gleam of pure malice in Eunice's eyes.

"Ms. Lerner?" I recognized the speaker as Joe Dresden, the chief of police. "We'd like to ask you a few questions—at the station."

I stared at him for an instant, startled. "Yes, sir," I said finally, and then, I went out with the two men. Joe Dresden's car was parked in front. He got in behind the wheel, and the other man sat beside me in the backseat.

There was a loud silence during that short drive. What had Eunice told them? Had Hugh changed his story? What would they ask me?

When we got there, he offered me a chair. I sank into it numbly.

Joe Dresden sat behind his desk. "You understand, Ms. Lerner," he said, "that while this is just routine, in connection with the Wyndham case, you should be aware that anything you say may be used against you."

I nodded, and he continued. "First of all, we're trying to clear up the question of Mr. Wyndham's activity last night. He seems to be protecting someone. Surely, a man doesn't just drive around all evening until midnight—alone. You can see that without anyone to support that statement, his position is—well, to say the least, precarious." He hesitated, his eyes holding mine. "Ms. Dwyer tells us that you might be able to help us. You worked late, I understand. Was Mr. Wyndham in the office, too?"

"No, he—" My voice sounded shrill. I swallowed and tried again. "He and the others left before Eunice did. I was alone until I left at eight-thirty."

"I see. And then, you went directly home?" His eyes slid downward and I followed the direction of his gaze—down to my hands, which were clenched so tightly that my knuckles were white. "You went directly home, Miss Lerner?" he repeated.

"Yes." Then the blurred memory became suddenly clear to me. A twig snapping. Light blazing. Laughter. And what we'd been saying just before. "—we'll be starving to be together again. But, we mustn't be, Hugh—ever again. Not as long as you have a wife."

"No," I whispered, lifting my eyes in panic to Joe Dresden. "I—I started to drive home. He was waiting out near my house—"

"Had you planned to meet him there?" he interrupted.

"No. He was just waiting. He told me that he wanted to talk to me. We left his car there, and we went for a drive in mine."

"Where?" he asked.

I hesitated, and a slow fire of shame spread through me. "Down by the lake," I admitted.

"You stayed in the car?" he persisted.

"No, we walked. Then, we sat by the lake and—talked. Some kids came by later—"

He leaned back, smiling. "I'm glad that you told the truth, Ms. Lerner. You see, those young people called me this morning after hearing the news broadcast. What did you do next?"

"We drove back to his car, but sat and talked for a while," I told him.

"For how long? What time did you go home, Ms. Lerner?" he asked.

It was eleven o'clock, my mind said, but suddenly, the terrible importance of the hour, of the very moment, screamed through me. Hugh had said that it had been midnight.

I looked straight at Joe Dresden. "It was midnight," I said.

He leaned forward, his eyes boring into mine. "Midnight? Be very sure, Ms. Lerner. At midnight, Hugh Wyndham shot his wife. Were you there?"

I gasped. There it was—the terrible truth in words! They knew! I put my hands over my face. I was shaking terribly.

"Were you with him until midnight?" Joe Dresden shouted at me.

I shook my head wildly. "No—no! It wasn't that late. I didn't know—I didn't dream he'd—I hadn't meant for him to—"

"To what?" he asked angrily.

I looked at him over my shaking fingers. His face was tense, waiting.

"I wasn't thinking of murder," I whispered raggedly.

Joe Dresden leaned back, letting his breath out slowly. "That's all," he said. "An officer will drive you back to your office."

A hand under my elbow helped me up. Somehow, I got back out to the car. If there were eyes staring at me, it didn't matter. Nothing mattered—not anymore. The world had crashed down around me and there was nothing left.

"If you'll drive in the back way, I'll get my car," I told the young officer.

I didn't go home. I knew that I couldn't go back to the office and face Eunice or Mr. Worthington. I wanted more than anything in the world to be in my own room, with the door locked against the world. But, I couldn't meet Anna's troubled, pitying eyes either—not yet.

I drove out toward the highway, and my mind was whirling in confusion. I tried to think about Hugh, about what he must be feeling, but all I could think of was: How could you, Hugh? How could you have killed her?

It was after five when I drove home. Roger's car was already there, one door half open—as though he'd been in too great of a hurry to slam it shut. I heard voices as I opened the door, but when I went into the living room, there was silence. They were both standing there, waiting for me. Neither of them spoke.

I saw the newspaper then. Wife of Executive Murdered, the headline read. Underneath was a subhead: Office companion admits illicit love affair.

"Well," I murmured, "I see you've got the latest news."

"Where have you been?" Roger burst out. "We've been worried sick about you."

I sighed. "I've just been driving." I felt my mouth twist. "That's what Hugh said—only he hadn't been driving at all. He was at home, killing his wife."

"Then you were with him last night?"

Roger's face was very white. I felt very sorry for him—and for Anna, and for Mr. Worthington, and for Steven, and for Hugh—and for me.

"Yes, I was with him." There was no use denying it. "Those kids—"

Roger's shoulders slumped. "Well, we're involved, I guess," he said bleakly.

I didn't go back to the office. Mr. Worthington called, urging me to come back—to carry on as normally as possible.

"You can't stay hidden away forever, you know," he said. "You'll be called as a witness in the preliminary hearing, and the trial, if there is one. Wouldn't it be better to face it, right from the start?"

"I can't, Mr. Worthington," I told him. "Thank-you, but I just can't. Not yet."

It was a few weeks before the preliminary hearing. The murder weapon still hadn't been found, but the authorities had said that they were sure that it would be found before the case came to trial. They seemed to think that they had plenty of evidence—even without the gun.

I was called as a witness. The thought of seeing Hugh again was frightening. How would he look? Would we be brought face to face? I had to shut my mind against it all, finally—just as I'd learned to shut my eyes to the compassion in Anna's, and to the helpless anger that I'd seen in Roger's.

Hugh was brought in after all the witnesses had been seated. He didn't look at anyone. His profile was toward me. I noticed that he was terribly gaunt, and that he was very pale.

The first witness was the doctor who had examined Janice's body. The police officers who had answered Hugh's call were next, testifying to the results of their investigation. They claimed that there had been no sign of an intruder at the Wyndham home—no unexplained fingerprints, no unidentifiable tire tracks, no neighbor who had heard or seen anything. There was nothing. Nothing to save Hugh.

Then, the teenagers testified. They said that they'd gone to the lake after the football game to hang out. They testified that they'd heard our voices, listened a while, and heard the names "Hugh" and "Kirsten." Then, they explained, one of them had stepped on a twig and the two people had jumped up from where they'd been lying on the grass. The kids had turned the flashlight in their eyes, then run off.

"Ms. Kirsten Lerner," the clerk called.

As I sat down, I looked directly at Hugh. For the first time, he lifted his eyes, and they looked straight into mine. In them was a strange expression, almost like pity. A shiver ran through me and I turned my eyes away. Why should Hugh be pitying me?

I told my story slowly, and my voice was so low that the judge asked me to speak up so that I could be heard.

"I told him that we must never be alone together again—not while he had a wife," I said.

"So, you were denying yourself to him until such time as he had—gotten rid of—"

"I object to the insinuation implicit in that question," Donald Emmons interjected angrily. "This is a hearing, not a trial."

"Mark the question off the record," the judge said. "The witness has been clear enough. Please continue, Ms. Lerner."

"Then he got out of my car—" I began.

The door at the back of the room burst open. I saw that a bailiff was trying to block someone's headlong rush. But, the person—a child—dodged past him and came forward, panting as though he'd had to fight his way in. It was Steven! He stopped at his father's side, threw his arms around his neck, and hung on.

"Daddy—Daddy!" Steven cried, kicking at the bailiff's shins. "Don't let them hurt you! They can't! You didn't kill her!"

Donald Emmons sprang to his feet, staring. The judge leaned forward.

"What's that boy doing in here?" he asked.

"Steven, how did you get in here?" Hugh was asking, his voice grim with horror.

"I ran away. I heard it over the radio, Daddy, about them keeping you in jail. I asked them to let me come home, but they wouldn't, so I ran away. I—I hitchhiked after I ran out of money. But, I had to come and tell everyone about—him."

No one was pulling on Steven now. Everyone was just staring at him.

"What do you mean, son?" Hugh asked. "There's nothing that you can do for me here." His stricken eyes turned to the judge, then to Donald Emmons. "Please, Donald," he begged brokenly.

Donald Emmons put a hand on Steven's shoulder, but Steven struck it away.

"You've got to listen!" he cried. "You've got to! Daddy didn't kill my mother. He did! I heard him say that he would!"

Donald Emmons turned to the judge. "The boy's right, Your Honor," he said. "We've got to listen."

"Yes," the judge said. "Step down, Ms. Lerner."

They let Steven stay right there with his father's arm around him.

"Steven," Hugh said, holding the child so that he had to look straight into his father's eyes, "this isn't like a movie or a television show. This is very serious. You mustn't make up a story—not at a time like this."

"I'm not, Daddy," Steven insisted. "I heard him say it."

"Heard who say what?" Hugh asked. "What are you talking about, Steven?"

"The man. The man that I saw with Mom that day—the day I ran away out to Ms. Lerner's barn."

I saw Hugh's face go white. His fingers clenched Steven's shoulders. "Steven, tell me—what did you see that day?" he asked firmly.

Still looking into his father's face, Steven told his story. "I left school and went home. I ran to Ms. Lerner's barn after I saw—them."

"Saw who?" Donald Emmons pressed.

Steven looked at him a moment, then turned back to his father.

"I went in the house and couldn't find Mom, so I went to her room. I opened the door, and I was trying to be really quiet so I wouldn't wake her. And, that's when I—I saw them." He shuddered. "I mean, Mom and the man—in bed."

"Steven!" Hugh gasped. "That—that isn't true!"

"But, it is true," he insisted. "I saw them—and then, I ran away."

For a long moment, there was dead silence in the room. Then someone coughed.

"But, Steven, that doesn't mean he killed your mother," Donald said gently.

"He came back the day Mom was packing my things for school," Steven continued. "They didn't know that I was there, but I hid, and I listened. Mom wanted to go away with him, and he didn't want her to. They yelled at each other. She said she was going to tell someone and he said that if she did that, he'd kill her. And then, I was so scared that I went to my room."

Hugh found his voice again then. "Steven, why didn't you tell me? Why did you keep all of that horror bottled up inside of you?"

Steven rubbed his sleeve across his eyes. "I guess I was scared," he admitted. "I thought if you knew you might get really angry. I didn't know what to do, Daddy."

Donald Emmons straightened his shoulders. His eyes were bright.

"I submit to you, Your Honor," he said, "that we have new

evidence that warrants a change in this hearing."

"Let's not get ahead of ourselves, Donald," the judge protested mildly. "There's new evidence, certainly—if the boy's story doesn't break down under questioning. But, we will release Mr. Wyndham under bond, pending investigation of this evidence. Hearing recessed until a later date."

I met Hugh's eyes over his son's head. They held a strange, unreadable expression. I hurried from the room before Steven could see me and wonder why his father wouldn't let him come to me.

They found the man in question in a matter of a few hours. Once they'd been given something definite to search for, they found plenty of evidence. Two letters which Donald Emmons claimed were "blackmail material" were found locked in a secret compartment of a small desk. There was a necklace that Hugh denied ever having paid for—or seen—which was traced to an out-of-state jeweler who remembered the purchase, and the purchaser.

And so, Michael Guerney was found. The gun he had was of the caliber that matched the bullets in Janice Wyndham's body.

It was then that the case against Hugh Wyndham was dismissed, and Michael Guerney, a prominent physician, was charged with first-degree murder.

For days, I sat in my room with the door locked. Anna came again and again and knocked, begging me to speak to her.

"Please, Kirsten—open the door! Please, come down and eat with us!" But, when I wouldn't, she'd bring a tray up and set it on a chair outside the door. I left the food there, untouched, until she'd taken it away again.

I faced myself with loathing, during those long days and even longer nights. By then, I understood more about love than I ever had before. I knew what a useless thing it was, unless it was supported by faith and loyalty. I knew that the emotion that I'd given to Hugh was not worthy of the name "love."

I learned about shame, too, and remorse, and self-contempt. And I learned about loneliness.

One day, Mr. Worthington called and told Anna to tell me that he needed me very badly at the office. He explained that he'd lost the girl he'd hired in my place and he was in a tight spot until he could find someone else. Hugh, he told Anna, had been transferred to another office.

So, at last I went back into the world—back to work. There was a man working in Eunice's place now. The other employees greeted me gladly, as though I'd just been away on sick leave.

Mr. Worthington took my hand in his and drew me into his office.

"I'm glad you came," he told me. "I've needed you. But, it's good for your sake, too, to stop running away. Everyone makes mistakes, Kirsten, and forgiving yourself is as necessary as forgiving someone else who has wronged you."

Tears flooded my eyes. "Don't be so kind, Mr. Worthington," I said. "I don't deserve it. I can't forgive myself—ever. And Hugh must hate me, too."

He smiled. "You didn't believe in Hugh's innocence when he was in trouble, and now you don't have any faith in his love."

"Hugh's not a fool, Mr. Worthington! How could he ever forgive me, or trust me again—or love me?"

"He has forgiven you, Kirsten, because he understands. As for the rest of it, we'll have to wait and see. Hugh is a fine man. If I were you, I'd spend the next few months trying to be as fine a woman." He gave me a warm smile. "How about it?"

A month later, I was a few minutes late getting to the office. When Mr. Worthington's buzzer sounded, I hurried in for our usual meeting. But, it wasn't Mr. Worthington who was sitting there. It was Hugh.

"Hello, Kirsten," he said calmly.

I gasped and felt for a chair to fall down into.

"Sorry I startled you," he said. "I asked Mr. Worthington to lend us his office. He told me about the talk that he had with you. I've done a lot of thinking, Kirsten. I needed to be sure just how I felt about everything—about you. Now I'm sure."

"Oh, I'm so ashamed, Hugh!" I exclaimed.

"I know," he said soothingly. "Believe me, I understand. The pressure was pretty intense. There didn't seem a chance that I was innocent. But, I did drive around during that hour after I left you. I did find Janice dead."

He shut his eyes for a moment, then opened them and smiled at me. "But, all of that's over now. We've both suffered enough. You know, Steven keeps talking about you, Kirsten. He wants a kitchen like the one you have at your brother's—one that smells like vanilla and warm bread and love. He wants a barn and a cow. And, I think he wants you." He put his hand out to me. "I want you, too."

The pounding of my heart was choking me. I put my hand in his. "Oh, Hugh," I whispered.

"We have the rest of our lives, Kirsten. All we need to do is to make a fresh start, and put the past behind us. What do you think?"

I know that I don't deserve another chance, but because Hugh's love is not weak like mine was, and because of his forgiving heart, I seem to be getting one. My heart is very full as I write this—it's overflowing with a constant prayer that, somehow, with God's help, I'll learn to be worthy of that second chance.

THE END

A KILLER IS STALKING
MY FAMILY
Will we be saved in time

I was ready for some big changes in my life. My family's move to a new area was the first. Not that moving to a new city was unusual for us. In fact, we did it all the time. My husband, Keith, had a job as a sales rep for a computer software company that kept him on the road constantly. Our thirteen-year-old daughter, Belinda, had already been to schools in twelve different states. But, I was excited that finally, our move would be different.

Keith had taken a permanent position in management and, we were settling down to stay. We'd settled on a home to rent with an option to buy, and we were pretty sure that we would end up buying the place. It would be a real home, not just a temporary place until it was time to move. We would be unpacking those boxes containing our household possessions one last time. I could hardly wait.

It had been tough on Belinda, always being the new kid in school. She was eager to "belong," never having been a part of the "popular crowd," and never having had a best friend for any length of time.

But, a more normal school life for Belinda and having Keith around more weren't the only reasons why I was so happy about the move. I was thrilled, at long last, to be pregnant again. I was expecting the arrival of our much hoped-for second child six months after we moved in. Keith and I had long ago resigned ourselves to the fact that we might never have more children when, suddenly, I'd missed a period. I'd rushed to the doctor and was soon able to call Keith on the road with the glorious news.

The first time that we'd caught sight of our new house, I'd known that it was the one for us. It was a beautiful old house, located on a heavily wooded lot. After years of apartment living, we were ready to spread out, and the five-bedroom house and big yard were a dream come true. Of course, we'd had no idea that just a few months after we'd moved in, our lives would be in danger and our world in utter chaos.

Belinda had actually thought that the house looked kind of spooky at first. I'd jokingly told her that maybe she'd been watching too many horror movies on TV. But, all it took was one look inside to convince her that we had picked the right house.

"Whoa, look at all this space!" she exclaimed, wandering from room to room on the first floor. "Awesome!" She ran upstairs to explore. Within minutes, she'd chosen her room—the one farthest away from the master suite. Given the volume at which she sometimes played her stereo, Keith and I were relieved.

The first of many of the peculiar things that would happen to us occurred on moving-in day. Keith was in the house wrestling with the furniture and Belinda was upstairs "arranging her space," as she'd put it. I was outside in the driveway, supervising the moving men and trying to keep track of the large boxes into which we had packed all of our worldly possessions.

I had just seen the last of the boxes marked "kitchen" on its way into the house and headed for the right room. I was standing on the porch when I saw a little girl walking across the lawn toward me.

"Hello," I said, admiring her pretty hair. She clutched a teddy bear that looked like he had been very loved, indeed. "Are you one of our new neighbors?" I asked.

She nodded and pointed to the house on our right. "I live over there," she said.

In just a few minutes, I'd learned that her name was Cara, that she was four years old, and that she had an older brother named Peter.

"Well, Cara, my name is Ellen," I told her. "My husband's name is Keith, and our daughter's name is Belinda." I didn't mention the new life growing inside me. For the time being, I'd decided that it would be my family's precious secret.

"Do you have any little kids?" she wanted to know.

"No, we don't. I'm sorry," I told her. "Belinda's thirteen. I'm afraid that's not very little. How old is your big brother?" I asked.

She rolled her eyes. "Oh, he's eight. He gets into all kinds of trouble!"

"Does he really? Well, hopefully, you don't," I said. "Maybe one day when we're all settled in, I'll make my famous oatmeal raisin cookies, and you and your brother can come over for a visit. I like little kids." I was eager to be acquainted with our new neighbors.

At my invitation, Cara had shook her head vigorously. "We're not allowed to go in that house," she whispered, pointing to our brand-new dream home. "Mommy told us that there are dead children in there."

I was stunned. What could she possibly have meant by such a bizarre remark? Why would a mother tell a child such a scary thing? I was just about to ask her for an explanation when I heard a woman's voice calling from next door.

"Cara! Come back here right this minute!"

The little girl's face took on a look of having been caught doing something that she wasn't supposed to have been doing. Without another word, she turned and scampered back across the lawn. I craned my neck, trying to catch a glimpse of Cara's mom, but I couldn't see past the hedge that the little girl had squeezed herself through.

I was a bit uneasy concerning Cara's strange remark about the dead children, I decided to go next door and introduce myself to the new neighbors as soon as we were settled.

About an hour later, as I walked into the garage, I noticed that some of the packing boxes were open. I went to investigate and was surprised to see a little boy digging into one of them.

"Hello!" I said. "Are you looking for something?"

Instead of being embarrassed to be caught snooping, he'd just shrugged. "Nah. You guys don't have any good stuff." Then, without a second glance at me, he'd walked out of the garage and through the hedge to the house next door. Somehow, I knew that I had just met Cara's big brother, the one she'd told me got into all kinds of trouble.

Well, I thought, he's off to a good start.

There was so much to do during the next few weeks—all of the things that went along with moving into a new home. Unpacking, putting everything away, hanging curtains, and lining shelves and drawers. The list of tasks seemed endless. More than once, I'd complained to Keith and Belinda.

"I can't believe that we still have so much stuff," I said. "We had a garage sale before we left our last apartment, and we still have so much to put away."

Eventually, I found the time to go over and introduce myself to our neighbors, whose children we had already met.

"Hi, Cara," I said as the little girl opened the door. "Do you remember me? I'm Ellen, the new neighbor from next door."

"Sure," she answered with a nod. "Did you bring any cookies?"

So, she'd remembered my promise! I regretted having arrived empty-handed and promised to bake some very soon.

"Is your mommy at home?" I asked.

"Yes." Cara nodded again.

Just then, a woman came to the door.

"Hello," I said, holding out my hand. "I'm Ellen Atherton from next door."

The woman hesitated. Reluctantly, she shook my hand and introduced herself as Tonya Devivo.

"Welcome to the neighborhood," she said. But, it seemed as though the greeting and her smile had seemed forced.

"Thank-you," I told her. "I think that my family will be very happy here."

"I hope that you will be," she told me finally, after a long pause. Her voice was dripping with doubt.

Suddenly, I'd remembered the odd thing that Cara had said, about there being dead children in our house. Surely, it had been just something that she'd heard in a scary movie. I decided not to mention it in front of the little girl.

Another awkward pause followed. I'd realized that Tonya Devivo was not going to invite me inside, something that I would have done. Maybe I'd caught her at a bad time. Still, I was embarrassed and, after mumbling something about how nice it had been to meet her, I'd walked back home. As I'd approached our front steps, I was stunned to see a little boy coming out the front door. It was the boy that I'd caught going through our boxes in the garage that first day.

"What were you doing in our house?" I asked. "You're Peter, I presume."

He smirked. "Yeah, that's me." He headed next door.

"Wait a minute!" I called. "I asked you what you were doing in our house."

"Just looking for spooks," he said.

I was stunned, yet I'd caught myself before I'd asked him if he had found any.

"Listen here, young man," I said. Anger was rising in my stomach, and it had made me feel queasy. "You have no business going into other people's houses, any time you feel like it, and looking through their things. If I catch you at it again, I'll have a talk with your parents."

Despite my words, he still wore a cocky grin. "My parents won't talk to you," he told me, sounding sure of himself. "Anyway, you won't be here for long."

Then, leaving me standing there with my mouth hanging open, he'd disappeared through the hedge.

During dinner that evening, I'd told my family about my first impression of the next-door neighbors. I'd said that the little girl talked about dead children, the boy was a snoop with a smart mouth, and that the mother was aloof. Not a very good first impression.

"I hope it isn't an indication of the neighborhood," Keith said.

"You know, some kids at school told me that our house is haunted," Belinda announced. It was as though she'd just remembered.

"Did anyone happen to elaborate on that comment?" Keith asked.

Immediately, I'd focused on Cara's dead children comment. And, I couldn't help but remember Peter's admission that he had been "looking for spooks."

"No, they seemed kind of uncomfortable when I asked," Belinda replied. "But, there's this one girl that I think I've really clicked with. I'll ask her."

Our daughter was too happy about the new friends that she was making in school to let anything bother her.

"Don't sweat that woman's cold welcome," she advised. "It took a while for people to start talking to me at school. I'm so psyched. For the first time, I finally feel like it's worth investing time in a friendship." She sounded older and wiser than her years. "There's even a guy who seems interested in me," she added.

And so, when she woke up the next morning complaining of a sore throat, she wasn't having any of my overprotective mothering. I'd told her that I wanted her to stay home and rest.

"No way," she insisted. "It's not that bad. And I don't want to miss a chance to talk to my new friends."

By that afternoon, I'd had a mild sore throat myself and had started wondering if Belinda and I were both catching something. Keith, though working overtime while getting settled in his new job, seemed healthy enough. Since it was a Friday, and I was feeling lazy right before the weekend, I'd decided that we would order pizza that night so I wouldn't have to cook dinner.

I was lying on the sofa, reading a novel, when Belinda came home from school that afternoon bursting with news.

"I found out why some kids say that our house is haunted," she announced breathlessly as she dropped her backpack on the floor near the front door.

"Why?" I asked.

"Because," she said, gasping as if she had run all the way home rather than taking the bus, "some little kids that used to live here died!"

"How?" I was almost afraid to hear her response.

"Nobody knows," she replied. "But the point is, it wasn't just one little kid, but two of them. Sisters, from the same family. Isn't that just too weird?" she asked.

"Well, it certainly is disturbing. I wonder how we can find out about it."

"I'll bet that lady next door knows," Belinda said. "Didn't that little girl say that she wasn't allowed here because of dead children?"

"That's what she said," I admitted. "But, I just thought it was something she heard in a movie."

"Maybe not. Maybe it's something that her mom actually said," she pointed out.

I talked it over with Keith when he got home that evening while we were waiting for the pizza to be delivered.

"Isn't the realtor obligated to inform a potential buyer if there were any suspicious deaths in the house?" I asked.

Keith didn't know. "The library should have all the newspapers on file," he said. "Maybe you can look up what happened."

47

It was a thought, although I had to admit that I didn't know quite where to start. I could just see myself at the library computer, typing in something like "dead children" and our new address.

When the doorbell rang, I grabbed my purse before answering the door. The pizza guy didn't look any older than Belinda. I knew that he had to be, if he were driving a delivery truck.

"Nobody's lived in this house for a long time," he informed me as he handed over the bill.

"Do you know why?" I took a stab at asking.

He seemed eager to share what he knew. "Some little kids who lived here a few years ago got sick and died. After that, two more families with kids have moved in here," he told me. "But, they both left suddenly after just a few months." The young man shook his head. "Spooky stuff," he remarked. "Do you have any little kids?"

My voice stuck in my throat and all I managed to do was shake my head. No, we didn't have any little kids. But what about my baby, that tiny new life that was growing inside of me?

I had little appetite for dinner after hearing the story, even though one part of me kept trying to convince myself that young people were often likely to exaggerate. And, everything he'd said was probably just hearsay, anyway. I promised myself that I would go to the library on Monday morning and look into the matter.

I pleaded my sore throat as the reason for my loss of appetite. In truth, the soreness had gotten steadily worse and I'd even gotten a nosebleed at one point in the day. I'd found myself feeling achy and tired, symptoms that could also be caused by my pregnancy— symptoms that I'd decided to keep to myself for the moment.

I was pleased to hear that Belinda's sore throat had improved throughout the day, and that she had shown no more sign of it. She and Keith chattered happily throughout the meal, thankfully failing to notice my brooding silence. Already, I felt as though the stories of the "dead children" had taken away from the thrill of our perfect dream house.

The next morning, Saturday, my throat was worse and so were the body aches. But I had a mountain of laundry to do, so I forged ahead. Keith and Belinda carried the two overflowing baskets downstairs to the laundry room.

"What's all that dirt on the wall?" Keith asked as I switched on the light.

I looked in the direction of his gaze. He was right: There, on the wall next to the washer, was a splatter of blackish green gunk. I knew very well that it hadn't been there when we'd moved in.

"How strange," I said, reaching for the spray cleaner and a roll of paper towels. The stuff cleaned up quickly and I didn't think any more about it as I did the laundry that morning. But, as I'd removed the last load from the dryer, I'd noticed a wet-looking patch on the throw rug that I'd put down in front of the appliances. I frowned into the empty washer and looked behind it.

Did my trusty washer spring a leak? I wondered. I'll ask Keith to take a look, I thought, picking up the rug and tossing it over the clothesline that was strung across the garage.

"This is a rainy area," he said later, and I remembered we'd had quite a downpour the night before. "I wonder if there's any way that the rain's seeped in from somewhere outside. I'll check around," he promised.

After I'd put away the laundry, I'd decided to let my increasing exhaustion get the better of me. I lay down for a nap on the family room sofa. But, I found Belinda lying there ahead of me, an afghan pulled up to her chin, watching music videos on TV.

"Hi, Mom," she greeted me as I walked in. "My sore throat's back," she added. "I feel kind of achy, too."

I followed my mother's instinct and felt her forehead. "You do feel a little warm, honey," I told her. "Why don't you take a couple of pain relievers and continue to rest? I'm feeling a bit under the weather myself. I'm going up to take a nap." I didn't want to roust her from her comfy spot. "Stay there, honey. I'll bring you the pain relievers and a glass of water, since I'm already up."

By Monday, Belinda and I were still feeling pretty rotten while Keith, luckily, felt fine. He insisted on taking off the morning to drive the two of us to the doctor's office. Sitting in the waiting room, watching the steady drizzle that fell outside the window, I'd complained about having to postpone my planned visit to the library.

"I think that your health and Belinda's is much more important," Keith insisted. I knew that he was right. "And the baby's," he added, reading my mind.

The doctor couldn't find anything specifically wrong with me, or with Belinda. Neither of us had a fever, and there was only a slight amount of redness in our throats, despite their soreness.

"It could be allergies," he told us. "You're new in town and there are probably all kinds of pollens out there that you've never been exposed to before." He recommended an over-the-counter allergy medicine. Although we stopped at the pharmacy and picked up some for Belinda, I knew that I wouldn't take any myself because of the baby.

After we got home, I went upstairs to try and take a nap. I found thoughts of the baby foremost in my mind. We had waited such a long time for me to become pregnant again. We'd almost given up hope by the time that it had actually happened. I was determined to take every precaution, and I had already read through several books on pregnancy. But, as I lay there, a pesky thought kept pushing its way into my mind. Once again, I couldn't help thinking about those poor, dead children who had supposedly once lived in our new home. I needed to learn more about them.

Suddenly, I had a thought. I decided that I would call the realtor. Surely, the person who had sold us the house would know all about the people who had lived there before. According to the pizza delivery boy, the last two families had only stayed for a short time. That meant that they had probably only rented the place. Had they considered buying it? And, had something happened to make them change their minds and leave?

I'd rushed down to the kitchen and flipped through my address book until I'd found the number. I was put through immediately to the woman who had shown us the house.

"Have you decided to go ahead with your option to buy already?" she asked, an air of confidence about her, once the pleasant greetings were out of the way.

"Not yet," I told her. "But, I've been curious about the former tenants. I wonder if you can help me."

She hesitated. "Well, you know that I can't give out any personal information," she said hesitantly.

"Look, Mrs. Hudson," I said, deciding to level with her, "I'm expecting a baby. The fact is, I've become disturbed about some rumors that we've heard about this house. I understand that children who've lived here in the past have become ill." I paused. "And, we've heard that some may have even died from their illnesses. Frankly, I think that you owe it to us, and to our unborn child, to tell us if anything strange and unhealthy has gone on here in the past." There was another long pause as she obviously considered my strong words.

"All right, Mrs. Atherton. I'll be honest with you. The last two families who rented that house did have young children. Kids under the age of ten, I believe. And, yes, the children were ill, but the doctors couldn't find anything wrong with them. No one knew what had caused them to get sick. Neighbors and local town gossip eventually brought up the subject of the two children who'd died there a few years before, and the families got scared and moved out." The realtor let out a long sigh. "That's why the price of the house has come down so much. It stood empty for a long time before you and your family moved in."

"Well, we've lived here for just a few weeks and already, both my thirteen-year-old daughter and I are sick," I told her. "The doctor is attributing it to allergies. We've never had trouble with allergies before."

"Well, this is a wet area and there are a lot of plants that grow out here that you might not be used to," she offered. It was the same story that I'd heard from the doctor.

"Can you put me in touch with the people who own the house?" I asked. "I'd also like to get in touch with the family that lost their children."

She wouldn't give me the owners' number directly, but promised to give them ours, along with a request to call us as soon as possible. She told me that she didn't know how to get in touch with the other family.

Belinda went back to school the next day. She told me that her throat felt no worse, and she explained that she didn't want to miss any more days.

I wasn't feeling great but I was tired of lying around. I decided to get back to working on the house. I wanted to get started on painting the room that we'd picked to be the baby's nursery—the room directly across the hall from the master bedroom. The room was empty since we didn't have any furniture for it yet, but the walls needed washing down.

I went down to the laundry room for cleaning supplies. Just before I'd walked into the room, I could have sworn that I'd heard the garage door close. But, when I peeked out, no one was there.

Maybe it's Peter, again? I thought. Why is he so interested in our house?

It didn't help my mood one bit to see that there had been a recurrence of the awful blackish-green gunk on the laundry room wall. That time, it had traveled all the way up to the ceiling, where it had begun snaking its way across the room in elongated fingers. I looked closely at the wall beside the washer. Were those handprints, or had the stuff actually spread that way? It was hard to tell. Could Peter have been playing a prank on us, trying to get us spooked? But, I couldn't see any way that he could have gotten it on the ceiling.

Where is this stuff coming from? And, how can it have spread so fast? Those were the burning questions in my mind as I once again scrubbed the wall clean, using a ladder and mop to reach up to the ceiling. In my weariness and frustration, I didn't even think about any danger to the baby until the job was done. Keith would have had a fit if he'd found out that I had been climbing a ladder.

I didn't get up to the nursery until the following day. My throat was still scratchy, but I was less tired. I flung open the door with new determination to wash the walls and to start painting.

There, along one wall, was the blackish green gunk that I had already scrubbed off the laundry room walls twice in less than a week. The offending slime snaked along in fingers that reached up to the ceiling, just as it had downstairs the day before.

The air felt thick, and I struggled to breathe. My eyes were stinging, and tears were running down my face. I felt as if a fist were clenched in the pit of my stomach, making me nauseous with fear. As I stood in the doorway, frozen in shock, I'd heard a sound and strained my ears to listen. Was it the faint sound of crying children? Surely, I was letting my imagination get the better of me. I had put a hand protectively over my stomach when, suddenly, I'd felt the bile rush up into my throat. I'd rushed to the bathroom just in time to be sick.

After I'd washed my face, I couldn't keep from going downstairs to the laundry room. I'd already suspected what I would find. There, just like the previous day, the walls and ceiling were smudged with slime.

I was lying on our bed when Belinda came home. "Are you okay, Mom?" she asked, coming in and plopping herself down in my dressing table chair. Without waiting for an answer, she went on. "You know what's weird? Every morning, I wake up with that same sore throat," she said. "But, by the afternoon, I notice that it's gone away. It's almost as if I catch it during the night and lose it at school. Weird, huh?"

I let my breath out in a long sigh. I was so tired that every bone and muscle seemed to ache.

"Not so weird, honey," I told her. "I'm just waiting for your dad to come home and then we're going to figure out what to do. But, I know one thing: Something is very wrong with this house."

She looked surprised. "Seriously? You mean, it's haunted, like the kids said?"

"I don't know about haunted," I told her, "although the nursery did have a rather poltergeist feel to it when I opened that door today."

When Keith got home, I showed him the rooms and related the entire story, except for the part about hearing the crying children.

"Frankly, I don't want to spend another night in this house," I told him.

"Neither do I," Belinda said, "if it's what's causing my throat to be sore."

I had worried that Keith would think that I was overreacting, but he took us both very seriously. Within half an hour, we had packed a few days' worth of clothes and headed for a motel. The following day, Keith had called the state's department of health. He'd also called our realtor to alert her to the possibility that we might not be staying, depending on what we discovered. He told her that he was deducting the cost of the motel from our rent payments, and that we would not be returning to the house until it was safe to do so.

Keith had consulted an attorney and had been told that we were within our rights to ask for what we had. Keith also told the realtor that she should notify the owners of the home immediately. My husband told me that she hadn't argued with him. She'd just said that everything would be taken care of.

Representatives from the health department went to the house during that week and checked out the dampness. They took samples of the slime on the walls.

When they reported back to us on their findings, I'd felt a little silly for not having thought of it before. The offending gunk was black mold. At first, they'd thought that the mold was a result of the rain and general dampness of the area. But, when the owner of the house came forward with the original blueprints, it turned out the laundry room had been built over an old well. The well had not been properly drained at the time of construction.

The mold had crept into the insulation for the laundry room and the room above—the room that we had planned to turn into a nursery. Eventually, with nothing to stop the spread of it, the dampness and subsequent mold had seeped into the insulation throughout the rest of the house.

The owner of the house had met with us and told us that he'd planned to take care of all the repairs, the draining of the old well, the replacing of the insulation, and the fresh paint. Then, he'd asked us if we still wanted to buy the house.

I'd asked him if it was his children who had gotten sick and died in that house, and he'd said no. Then I asked him a question that some may have thought harsh, but which I'd thought was appropriate.

"If it had been your children, would you have investigated into the matter sooner, rather than continuing to rent a house that was making people sick?"

He'd hung his head. He'd had no answer.

We didn't buy the house, although we'd decided that we did want to stay in the area. After all, Keith had his new job, and Belinda was making friends at school. We ended up buying a smaller house—one that would be a lot less maintenance. We had it thoroughly checked out beforehand, including an investigation by the environmental health and safety department, as well as the Center for Disease Control and Prevention. The peace of mind that we'd felt about moving into the new house had made it well worth the extra effort.

Keith was the only one who even went back to that old house. Belinda and I wouldn't set foot in it. He'd hired movers to take care of all our things. We ended up leaving a lot of it behind on professional advice. We didn't want to take the chance that the mattresses and sofa and chairs might have been infected in just the short amount of time that we'd lived there.

We filed suit against the home's owner and so did the other families who had gotten sick while living there. We even met the family who had lost the two children, little girls named Isabella and Katie Lynn. My heart ached for them, and I could only imagine the pain that they had suffered.

Belinda and I have been in great health since we left the house and so has Keith, even though he was lucky enough to have an immune system that the black mold hadn't been able to compromise. We don't talk about the other house often.

I needed to do one thing to help me bring about a sense of closure. I felt that I had to visit the graves of little Isabella and Katie Lynn. As I lay the flowers next to the small headstones, I'd felt the baby kick. I thought of the baby boy who was due any day. All the tests have indicated that our son will be a healthy baby.

I'll never know for sure if I really did hear children crying in the nursery that day. But, I said a silent prayer of thanks for whatever force had warned us to get out, before it was too late.

THE END

MY SON STOPPED A KILLER

My husband, Nick, had a stressful job—but then, so did most people. The problem with him was that he'd ever learned how to deal with problems in a positive way. I learned that early in our relationship, but I hadn't paid enough attention to the signs that should have been red flags. If I'd known then what I know now, I would never have married the man who nearly killed me.

From the very beginning or our marriage, Nick tried to control me. I couldn't do anything right. He griped about my housekeeping, my cooking, and my looks. "You're letting yourself go, Bella. I don't want a homely wife."

From the very beginning of our marriage, Nick tried to control me. I couldn't do anything right. He griped about my housekeeping, my cooking, and my looks. "You're letting yourself go, Bella. I don't want a homely wife."

So I started getting up early and putting on makeup. I worked out at least an hour a day. Still, he didn't seem satisfied.

"I want a kid," he barked one night. "Everyone has kids except me."

I wanted children, too, but I had some serious concerns about my marriage. However, over time, I thought about it. I rationalized that maybe having a child with Nick would help our marriage.

After Alfonso was born, I noticed how Nick's bad temper had gotten much worse. Instead of cussing, ranting, and raving about things that annoyed him, he began to swing his arms around. Sometimes, he even punched at the nearest object. By the time Alfonso was a year old, there wasn't a wall in our entire house that didn't have a hole in it!

Nick didn't hit me, but his violence still scared me. I didn't have anyone to talk to because my parents didn't like him, and I wasn't about to let them know they'd been right when they told me marrying him was a huge mistake. And because of Nick's control issues, I didn't have any close friends.

My fear of my husband kept me quiet when he went on a rant after a bad day at work. I did everything in my power to keep things nice for him at home. From the moment he left for work until he walked back through the door, I cleaned, cooked, and cared for baby Alfonso. Although Nick hadn't struck me yet, I didn't want to take any chances—especially with the baby.

Alfonso was my pride and joy, and I knew he depended on me

for safety and security. My hope for a better marriage was shattered when I realized having a baby only added more pressure, and Nick was meaner than ever.

I thought about getting a job and leaving Nick, but the thought of leaving my infant in day care sent a chill through me. I couldn't imagine a stranger being responsible for my son. Besides, my work skills were limited, and after paying for day care, it wouldn't be worth it. I didn't know any private sitters, so that was out of the question.

If my dad hadn't been out of work, I probably would have given in, taken Alfonso, and gone to my parents' house to live. But I knew they couldn't afford another couple of mouths to feed with my dad on unemployment and no signs of things letting up. My mother had arthritis, so she wasn't able to work on a regular basis. She took temp jobs when she felt well, but those times were becoming more and more rare.

Sometimes, Nick could be sweet—especially after a big tirade that made me cry. I was always surprised and hopeful that things would change whenever he acted remorseful. I'll ever forget how, after punching his fist through a wall, a startled expression covered his face, and he sank to the floor—sobbing. I cradled him in my arms, and he cried on my shoulder for a solid hour, while Alfonso lay sleeping in his crib. I was thankful he hadn't awakened during the awful event.

"I'm so sorry, Bella," Nick said between sobs. "I don't know what came over me. My job is stressful, and I hate my boss, but I shouldn't take it out on you."

"Why don't you apply for a job at another utility company?" I asked. "Maybe you'll get a better boss with a company that won't put so much stress on you."

Shaking his head, he replied, "You know I can't do that. My company is the highest paying one in town. There's a waiting list of electricians just waiting to take my place. Remember how long I waited, and how happy we were when they finally called me?"

"Yes, I remember," I said. "But is it worth it?"

"When it's time to pay the bills, it is."

I inhaled deeply, then slowly let out a sigh. Nick was right. Our bills were extremely high—especially after Alfonso's difficult birth. We had health insurance, but the deductibles were more than my husband's annual salary. As it was, it would take many years to pay it off. His company was self-insured, so the benefits weren't good.

We held each other as images of my marriage turning around, flitted through my mind. Maybe this would be the turning point, I thought.

When Alfonso began to cry, I stood up and went straight to him.

56

Nick sniffled, and he said I loved the baby more than I loved him. I tried arguing with him, but it was in vain. I'd figured out that my husband was jealous of our child, and there was absolutely nothing I could do about that.

Things got a little better over the next several months, until Nick got injured on a job. He had to take a short disability leave. We had income, but there was no overtime like we'd gotten used to. It put a serious crimp in our budget.

"As soon as Alfonso is in school, I'll go back to work," I offered a year later, hoping to relieve some of the pressure after another of his temper tantrums.

"I don't want my wife working," he snapped. "I need someone here to take care of my house."

"You won't even know I'm gone," I said. "I'll work part-time, and I'll be home in time to cook your dinner, and clean the house."

"Not in this lifetime," he said as he left, slamming the door shut behind him.

Since Alfonso was still several years away from starting kindergarten, I dropped the subject, figuring there was no point. Maybe Nick would change his mind later when he realized how much easier life would be if I contributed to the family income.

The years went by, but Nick didn't change. If anything, he became more adamant about my not working.

"I make perfectly good money," he said. "You just need to learn how to do a better job of budgeting. How much do you spend on groceries?"

After I told him, he cut the grocery budget in half. "You can't do that," I said. "As it is, I have to buy generic brands, and I can't get Alfonso some of the foods he really likes."

"He's not missing anything. Just deal with it."

Nick's tone let me know there was no arguing. He was firm, and if I continued to push, I'd have to deal with his temper—which I'd learned to avoid by not talking much.

One afternoon, after Alfonso started kindergarten, I met Maisie—another mom—while waiting outside for our children. She and I struck up a conversation, and I learned she had a great part-time job working in a call center. They were flexible with her hours, and she made decent money.

"They're always looking for more part-timers," she told me. "If you ever want to go back to work, just let me know. I'll get a referral bonus if they hire you."

Over the next several weeks, we got to know each other better. She was always right there to pick up her child, on time for the final kindergarten bell. I always saw a smile on her face, and she seemed extremely happy.

"It's the job," she told me. "Ever since I went back to having my own paycheck, I've felt more complete. I love being Erin's mom, but when she's in school, I feel so lost. I've never been one for shopping or sitting around watching TV. This gives me something constructive to do, and I even have my own bank account!"

That night, I decided to feel out Nick, and see if he'd changed his mind.

"What would you think if I got a very part-time job—say ten hours a week?" I asked. "Nothing around here would change at all."

"How many times do I have to say no?" he hollered, standing up from the table, sending his chair flying a few feet behind him.

I quickly glanced over at Alfonso, who stared down at his plate and shoved his peas around. He'd seen his dad's horrible temper before, so he wasn't too shocked. Still, though, I knew it upset him.

"Okay, okay," I quickly said to keep the peace. "I won't bring it up again. I just thought I'd ask."

"Don't ever ask me again," Nick said. "The answer always has been—and will always be—no!"

I accepted this for another couple of months, but when I asked if I could buy some new sheets for Alfonso's bed, Nick's reaction pushed me into making a decision that I knew would make him blow.

"What does he need character sheets for?" Nick yelled. "His plain blue sheets are perfectly fine. I won't have you spending my hard-earned money on something that ridiculous!"

"Your hard-earned money?" I said right back, instantly realizing I'd just flipped his temper switch. Okay, so now that I'd done it, I figured I might as well follow through. "I work hard, too. I'm home all day taking care of the house, cooking your meals, doing your laundry."

"Humph," Nick said, shaking his head and surprising me that he wasn't hollering even louder. "Anyone could do what you do, Bella. Don't give me that."

"Wait just a minute," I volleyed, feeling a boldness that was sure to cost me later. But he'd insulted me, and I couldn't just sit back and take it. "If anyone could do it, why do I have to stay home all day? I can go out and get a job, so we can afford some things that we want."

Now I could see the anger flickering through his eyes. Stabbing his finger in my chest, he pushed me back. "You don't need anything. Stop talking about getting a job, or you'll be sorry."

I bit my lips to keep from saying something that would totally push him over the edge. If Alfonso hadn't been home in his room, I might have taken my boldness to the next level. But I did worry about him witnessing too many of his father's tantrums.

"Say one more word about it, Bella, and I'm not kidding. . . ."

58

His voice trailed off, but that was okay. He didn't have to finish his sentence. His message came through loud and clear.

However, the next morning, I was back in the frame of mind to take action. I took Alfonso to school, then I stopped off at the place where Maisie told me she worked. After sitting in the parking lot working on my courage, I finally sucked in a breath, got out of my car, and marched toward the front door.

The front of the building was mostly glass. Once inside, I saw stark, light gray walls and tile floors made to look like marble. The reception desk was on the wall, facing the front door. As I walked toward the woman sitting there, the sound of my shoes echoed through the massive room with the tall ceiling.

"May I help you?" she asked.

I swallowed hard, squared my shoulders, and forced a smile. "I'd like to fill out an application for a job," I said.

She smiled and told me to hold on a minute. I watched her as she lifted her phone, punched in a few numbers, and mumbled that she was sending someone back to human resources. After she hung up, she gestured as she gave me directions.

My heart hammered in my chest the whole way up to the third floor, where I'd been instructed to go to the main desk to the right. I felt a strange sense of exhilaration combined with fear.

Although I knew Nick would be furious, I now knew that what would please me most in the world—besides something wonderful happening to my son, of course—was to have my very own job with my very own paycheck. Then I could buy things without having to ask permission. With Nick's tight budget, there was ever room for treats or fun food for Alfonso or me. Alfonso and I were lucky to have bologna sandwiches. If I got this job, I could send him to school with lunch money, and he could have the full school experience.

After I filled out an application, I was called into the interviewer's office. She was a nice lady who smiled often, and she encouraged me to tell her about myself. We discussed how I hadn't worked in a very long time, but she said that wasn't a problem for the job I was applying for.

"This company understands the needs of families," she said. "We're willing to work with you and your schedule because we want you to be happy and content in your job."

As I listened to her going on and on about how much the company focused on its employees, I just knew this was the perfect place for me to work. At the end of the interview, we stood up and shook hands.

"I'll call your references and get back with you in the next day or two," she told me before I left.

I was on pins and needles for two days—until my phone finally rang. "We'd like to offer you a position with our company," the woman from human resources said. "Can you start on Monday?"

"Yes!" I said.

We chatted for a few minutes about the new employee orientation and training, then we hung up. As soon as I got off the phone, an awful feeling flooded my veins. Nick would be furious.

For several hours, I went back and forth between worry about what Nick thought and excitement over my first new job in many years. I loved the fact that I'd impressed the human resources lady enough to make her want me working for her company.

Finally, I decided I'd do the job and not tell Nick—at least not for a while. He didn't have to know. I'd be there when he got home from work, and nothing would change around the house.

On Monday, as soon as I dropped Alfonso off at school, I went straight home and changed into nice slacks, a shirt, and a jacket. I wasn't sure of the dress code, so I figured I'd play it safe.

At orientation, I learned that I could wear jeans as long as they weren't tattered or stained. That was a good thing because if I started dressing up all the time, Nick might have become suspicious.

Over the next two weeks, I became more and more excited because I caught on very quickly. The trainer even commented that she'd ever seen anyone so eager and enthusiastic. I let her know I was thrilled to have gotten the job, and that I was determined to do well.

"I have no doubt you'll do as well as you want," she said with a smile. "I can even see you eventually going into management."

That made me feel even better. Just think. Management. Me. Wow! That boosted my confidence to a whole new level.

Once my training class got on the phones to actually talk to customers, the job was even better. We were offered an incentive if we "up-sold" to customers, so I made that my goal—to up-sell to everyone I spoke to. I had the highest numbers in the class, and the sales supervisor rewarded me for it by giving me a gift certificate to a nice restaurant.

Although most people would have taken their spouse out to dinner, I knew I couldn't even mention it to Nick since he still didn't know about my job. So I talked to Maisie, the woman who'd told me about the job.

"I'd like to take you out to lunch," I told her.

"Oh, you don't have to, Bella," she said. "Take your husband instead. You've worked hard for it, and I'm sure he'd be proud of you."

"I can't," I admitted. "I haven't told my husband I'm working."

"What?" she said, her face scrunched in confusion. "Why

wouldn't you tell your husband you're working?"

I shrugged sheepishly. "My husband's sort of old-fashioned about women working. He thinks I need to stay home and forget about making money."

"That's not old-fashioned," she said with a snort. "That's archaic."

"Yeah, I know," I admitted.

"Okay," she finally said. "I'll go to lunch with you. In fact, I consider it an honor. Did you know all the team supervisors are talking about what a great job you're doing?"

"Really?" I shrieked.

"Yes," she said with a smile. "And I even got a little bonus when they hired you."

"We're really working for a great company," I told her. "I love the way they reward people who do a good job."

"Yeah, me, too."

Maisie and I became pretty good friends over the next couple of months. She was the only person I could talk to about my job. She gave me some tips on how to streamline calls, and we shared call experiences. It was fun to have a work buddy with whom I could bond. I also told her how I was still struggling to keep my job a secret from Nick.

"How you're keeping this a secret from your family is beyond me," she said. "What will you do this summer when Alfonso is out of school?"

I shook my head. "I haven't thought about that yet."

"We have a day care on site, and they do fun things with school age children during the summer," she told me. "But if you bring Alfonso, you can't very well expect him to keep it a secret from his dad."

"In that case, I'll probably have to tell him by summer."

She reached out and gently touched my arm. "If you need me, you know you can call anytime."

"Thanks," I said.

The very next week, Alfonso woke up with a tummy ache, and I couldn't send him to school with a good conscience. I felt awful for him, but I also worried about calling in sick. After Nick left for work, I carried the cordless phone to the back of the house and called my supervisor. She was wonderful.

"All of us have kids," she said, "so we understand. If you need a few days off to stay home with your son, just let me know first thing each morning."

I blew out a sigh of relief. My job truly was a blessing. Not only did I now have my own money, I had a great boss who recognized my need to be a good mother. If only Nick would listen to me, and keep an open mind—but I knew he wouldn't. The instant I told him I had a job, I had no doubt he'd hit the roof. And maybe he'd hit me.

His violence was becoming more and more evident. His eyes sparked with rage as he came toward me after a particularly bad day, but he always stopped short of physically hurting Alfonso or me. I knew it was only a matter of time before he'd snap.

Alfonso stayed home from school one more day, but then he was able to return to school. I went to work feeling great to be out of the house again. Once I'd gotten used to going somewhere everyday besides the grocery store, I had a hard time staying cooped up in the house all day.

A few times, Nick said something about me not being home when he called. I had a different excuse each time, then I plied him with his favorite dessert or offered him another beer. His attention was fairly easy to divert—since I'd learned as long as I took care of his selfish nature, I was off the hook.

As summer drew near, I dreaded the prospect of having to talk to Nick. But it was inevitable. Time kept marching faster and faster, until I knew I had to say something.

Finally, we were three weeks away from the summer, when I told Nick I had something to discuss with him. "Not now," he growled. "There's a baseball game on TV."

I bit my tongue to keep from saying anything else. Instead, I nodded. "Later, then. But we really need to talk."

He narrowed his eyes before standing up and walking out of the kitchen, leaving Alfonso and me alone. I heard him go into the living room and turn on the TV. Alfonso finished his dinner, and he asked to be excused. I told him to get ready for bed.

As the game progressed and Nick got inebriated with beer, I worked on building up the nerve to talk to him about my job. Finally, he reached for the remote and punched the "off" button.

"You wanna talk," he said, gruffly. "So talk."

"Well," I began as I sat on the edge of the sofa. "You know how I've been wanting to work. . . ." I let my voice trail off so I could get a reaction from him.

He was very still for a few seconds before he shook his head. "Absolutely not. I don't know how many times I have to tell you: no wife of mine is gonna work."

"But—" I began before he cut me off.

"I said no, and I mean it." He stood up to leave, then he turned to me. "I'm the man of this house, and my word is final."

That did it. Something inside of me snapped. I stood up, walked right up to my husband and stared him down, until my voice kicked in. Then I said, "Too late, Nick. I have a job."

"You what?" he hollered.

"Don't wake Alfonso. I said I have a job. I have for months."

"Is that why you haven't been home when I called?"

I nodded. "But I always get my house work done. I'm there for Alfonso, and I have all your meals on the table."

Suddenly, I watched as he clenched his fists into tight balls. His jaw tightened, and his face flushed a deep shade of red. Then he blew. A steady string of cuss words flew from his mouth, and his arms began to flail.

"Calm down, Nick," I begged. "It's just a little part-time job. I'm able to buy your favorite desserts now. I can get you and Alfonso nice presents without having to ask you for money. You should be happy about it."

There was no reasoning with my husband. He was like a wild, angry animal. He told me he'd rather not have a wife than one who works. His words began to scare me when he said, "Where's my gun?"

"Your gun?" I asked in disbelief. "Don't you remember we got rid of it when we had Alfonso?"

He glared down at me before he stomped off to the kitchen. I assumed he'd gone in there to get more beer, so I took advantage of his absence to go back to our bedroom. However, I'd been there less than a minute when I heard him open the door and then slam it shut. To my shock and horror, he was wielding a knife, coming toward me with slow, steady strides.

"What are you doing, Nick?" I screamed. "Why do you have that knife?"

"Mommy," I heard from the bedroom door.

Oh no! We'd awakened Alfonso. My heart hammered in my chest as I watched Nick turn on his heel and move toward our son.

"What are you doing, Nick?" I shrieked. "Leave Alfonso alone! He's just a little boy."

Then he turned back to me. "You don't deserve to live," he said. He staggered for a moment, but he quickly regained his footing. He came toward me, an evil look in his eyes.

Next thing I knew, Nick had closed in on me. He had me pinned against the wall and hesitated only for a split second before driving the knife into my shoulder. I didn't feel the pain at first, but then he stabbed again—this time in my arm. That one hurt.

"No, Daddy, don't!" Alfonso screamed as he came running toward us. "Don't kill Mommy!"

"Go away, Alfonso!" I hollered. "Go call the police!"

The frightened look in Alfonso's eyes hurt me more than the

stabs that kept on coming. "But Mommy, I want to help you."

"Call . . . " I was growing weaker by the minute as Nick kept stabbing like a crazed maniac. I tried to finish my sentence, but the words wouldn't come. Then suddenly, my legs became numb, and they could no longer hold me up. I slithered down the wall, and I fell into a heap on the floor. I was barely conscious. I could hear, but I couldn't speak.

"No, Daddy," I heard Alfonso holler.

Next thing I knew, my son screamed as Nick told him one of us would live through the night. The muted sounds of the knife stabbing someone sent me into the worst tormented state I've ever experienced in my life. I knew my child was being stabbed by my husband. And it was all my fault.

I drifted in and out of consciousness as the house grew very quiet. Was I the only one still alive? Then I heard Alfonso's crying.

"Alfonso," I whispered, hoping my son could hear me.

"Mommy," he sobbed. "Daddy killed both of us."

"No, honey, Daddy didn't kill us. We're still alive."

"But he stabbed you to death."

"Did he hurt you?" I asked.

"Yes, he stabbed me to death, too." He sobbed a little more before adding, "Then he stabbed himself in the heart. He's dead. We're all dead."

It was growing increasingly difficult to talk, so I had to speak quickly. "Alfonso, honey, can you reach the phone?"

There was a brief pause before he replied, "Yes, Mommy, I have the phone right here."

"Call 911, okay?"

I listened as he pushed the numbers and spoke into the phone. "My daddy killed me and my mommy."

Then he clicked off the call. "Alfonso," I said with even more difficulty. "Call 911 again, and tell them where we live."

He did as he was told. "My mommy said to call you back and tell you where we live." Then he gave our address. There was a brief pause before he said, "I don't want to talk to you. My daddy killed me and my mommy."

"Honey, stay on the phone," I whispered. It hurt to talk, but I had to keep Alfonso on the phone for his sake. I might've been about to die, but I wanted him to live.

Alfonso didn't stay on the phone very long before I heard sirens. "Can I hang up now?" he asked.

"No," I said softly.

Next thing I knew, there was pounding on the door. Then came the sound of shattered glass and loud male voices. "I think they're back here," one of the men said.

64

I don't remember anything after that. When I awoke, I was in a sterile, white room with machines and humming sounds all around me.

When I tried to look around, I realized my head wouldn't move. Then I tried to speak, but my mouth wouldn't open. It took me a little while to realize where I was. The lady with the white smock on and the nurse's name badge clued me in very quickly.

She glanced over her shoulder and said, "She's awake." Then she turned to me. "You're one very lucky woman. Your little boy is fine; so don't worry about him. We just have to concentrate on getting you healthy again and back on your feet."

I'd been rendered immobile, so I wasn't able to talk or move any part of my body. I had to just lie there and let other people call the shots. One thing I noticed was that no one had said a word about Nick. I thought that was strange.

After what seemed like forever but was probably less than a week later, a nurse came in and took the vise off my jaw. "Some men from the police department are here to talk to you. They've been trying to get in here since you first arrived, but the doctor is just now giving them permission."

She took my hand, looked me in the eye, and added, "But only if you're ready to talk."

I tried to work my jaw, but it hurt, so I had to talk through closed teeth. "Talk about what?"

She closed her eyes before looking at me. "You don't know, do you?"

"Know what?"

"Do you remember anything about what happened?"

I did remember. In fact, that was all I'd been able to think about since lying here unable to move or communicate.

"Yes," I finally said, "I remember."

"The police want your story. They have to have the information before they can close their files."

"Close their files?" I said. "What do you mean by that?"

She backed away as she replied, "Let me go get the doctor. I'm not sure how to do this."

The doctor arrived a few minutes later. I watched her as she moved around the bed, studying the monitors, and checking the machines. I suspected that was to stall for time. Eventually, she moseyed over to my bedside.

"Hi, Bella," she said in a very unnatural voice. "Feeling a little better?"

"What's going on with the police?" I asked, my teeth still tightly shut.

She pursed her lips as she thought it over, then she blurted, "They want the details about the attempted murder. Your son has already talked, and now they want your side of the story."

"How about Nick? Are they hearing his side, too?"

"No, I'm afraid they can't do that. Nick died shortly after he got here."

All sorts of weird feelings flooded me. I was shocked at first, then I felt sad. That was quickly replaced by an odd combination of relief and anger.

"That little boy of yours is one brave kid," she added. "He's a little fighter."

"Is he okay?" I asked. "Did he get . . . stabbed, too?"

She forced a slight smile and nodded. "Yes, unfortunately, your husband managed to stab Alfonso a few times, but one of his vital organs got punctured. He'll have scars on his shoulder and arm, but besides that, he'll be good as new."

Silence fell between us as I took it all in. My son and I were going to be okay—without Nick. Why didn't I feel bad about that? What I felt was a sense of freedom and hope for the future.

Then guilt set in. Nick had died. It wasn't supposed to be this way. When we'd gotten married, I'd imagined having children and living happily ever after.

But the reality of it was, almost immediately after the wedding, I saw Nick for who he really was—a domineering man who didn't care about anyone but himself. If he couldn't have things his way, then no one would be happy. He created drama in his life—and mine—to get and maintain control.

"When can I see Alfonso?" I asked, my voice barely above a whisper.

"When you're up to it," she replied. "And after you talk to the police."

I swallowed hard. The police. Yes, of course, I needed to talk to them. A crime had been committed.

Squeezing my eyes shut, I tried to block out the mental images that were just now starting to surface. Remembering Nick as he came after me with the knife sent a chill of fear through me. But the very thought of him stabbing our son replaced that fear with anger. I needed to have closure on this and to see my son.

I opened my eyes and looked the nurse squarely in the eye. The exchanged glance was one of deep understanding and compassion.

"I'm ready to talk to the police," I said softly. "You can send them in now."

Fortunately, the police officer they sent in to talk to me was soft-spoken and gentle. She had a way about her that spoke of kindness.

"How long had he been abusing you?" she asked.

I started to tell her this was the first time, but she wasn't just talking about physical abuse. She needed to know.

During the next several minutes, I told her how my husband had started out making me feel unworthy of his love. Then he'd graduated to controlling every minute of my life. It had gotten so bad, I'd lied to him about my job out of fear for my safety—something I now knew. I'd instinctively hidden the fact that I'd gotten a job because I knew there would be consequences.

After she asked a few more questions, she thanked me and gave me her card. "If you need anything at all, or if you remember something you forgot to tell me today, call me. I want to make sure you're okay."

The nurse brought Alfonso in to see me as soon as the police officer left. His eyes were as big as saucers when he walked up to my bedside.

"Mommy?" he asked, hesitating before the nurse nudged him forward.

"Hi, honey. Are you okay?"

He nodded. "I've been staying with Grandma. She's nice, but I want to go home."

I glanced up at the nurse who hovered directly behind him. "When can we go home?" I asked.

She smiled as she gently laid her hand on Alfonso's shoulder. "It'll be a few more days, sweetie. We have to make sure your mommy is okay."

"Did she die?" he asked.

"No, honey," the nurse replied. "You were such a brave little guy, you saved your mommy's life. We're very proud of you."

Tears sprang to my son's eyes as he jerked out of her grasp and threw himself across my bed. The nurse looked horrified, but I smiled back at her and nodded that it was okay. I carefully stroked my son's hair as he sobbed into my sheets.

Knowing how badly my son missed being home with me, I cooperated fully and let the hospital staff know that it was important for me to get home as quickly as possible. When they sent me home, it was with explicit instructions to call if anything went wrong with the wounds they'd painstakingly cared for. My mom came to stay with us until I was able to move about freely.

"Why don't you sell your place and come to live with us for a while?" my mother asked after she dropped Alfonso off at school the second day I was home. "At least for the summer."

"I'm not sure I want to," I said. She and my dad were still struggling, although it was nice to know I had a safety net if nothing

67

else worked out. "As soon as I'm better, I want to go back to my job. My supervisor called me at the hospital and told me to come in when I was ready."

"I don't know if it's such a good idea to rush things," she said.

"It'll be good for me. I need to work and not only for the money. It's good for my sanity."

"But what about Alfonso?" she asked.

"They have day care on-site. He can go there in the mornings, while I work part-time. Then when school starts back, I'll see if they can switch me to full-time."

"Won't this be hard on you?"

"Not any harder than anything else. I like my job."

She thought it over, smiled, and nodded. "Yes, I know, honey. And I want you to be happy."

Now, eight months later, my life has gotten on a somewhat even keel. Things have been a little rough financially, but with Nick's life insurance from work, the social security income, and the salary from my job, I've been able to make ends meet. My medical bills are staggering, and I have to pay twenty percent of them. Dealing with Nick's insurance company hasn't been a piece of cake, so I had to hire an attorney as a middle man.

I'm very sad about how things turned out with Nick, but I'm grateful my son is turning out to be such a great kid. He is truly a hero—not only because he saved my life but also because he's a survivor. He's smart and seems to have a good sense of right and wrong. No mother could ask for any more than that!

THE END

HIT-AND-RUN KILLER
I can't let my husband find out

I think that everyone, at some point in their lives, makes a split decision that they instantly regret.

But, sometimes, that split decision isn't so easily undone. In the case of my split-second decision, I believed that I had everything to lose, and that my silence would harm no one.

Oh, how wrong I was.

Let me start at the beginning, so that you will get a better understanding of my horrifying story.

I'd been working as a bartender when I met my husband. I'd told him about my past—or most of it. It was the part that I hadn't told him that eventually came back to haunt me.

The part about my drinking, that is.

I didn't think that I was an alcoholic—just a coward. Basically, I had always been a shy person, and alcohol had always given me the added confidence that I'd needed when I'd had to deal with any major happenings in my life. But, I could go for months without drinking—sometimes years. I supposed that's why I didn't really consider myself an alcoholic.

And, that was why I had never told Conner, my husband, about my penchant for using alcohol to bolster my courage—or, about my previous DUI offense. When I'd seen him walk through the door into the bar where I'd worked, I'd felt something tug at me. It was almost as if someone had tied a string to my heart and attached it to his.

Since I worked in a bar, it wasn't unusual for me to see good-looking guys by the dozen. More than a few had hit on me, even though I didn't consider myself anything to get excited about.

Conner took a stool at the bar and ordered a soda, of all things. I'd thought at first that he was a cop, but he didn't look tough enough, in my opinion.

He was handsome, though—no doubt about that. He had the eyes of every girl in the bar on him, even the ones that were married, or there with dates. His smile would have made a nun have erotic dreams.

Imagine my surprise when he told me that he was a preacher. And, while I was struggling to unglue my tongue from the roof of my mouth, he pulled out a stack of inspirational brochures and placed them on the bar.

His voice was deep and soothing—like ocean waves washing

against the beach. "Care if I leave these?" he asked, immobilizing me again with his gorgeous smile.

I licked my dry lips and managed to nod.

"Sure, you can leave them." It never occurred to me to tell him that he couldn't. I wondered if anyone was able to refuse him anything. I had a good idea then of how a cult leader could entice people to mass suicide—at least, if the cult leader looked anything like that man.

"Thanks. Do you go to church anywhere?" he asked.

In my muddled mind, I considered lying. I wanted the man to like me—to think that I was a good person. I felt that, deep down inside, I was a good person. I believed that it was life and circumstances that had shaped my ugly past.

But, I found that I couldn't lie to a preacher, no matter how badly I wanted to impress him.

"No, I don't," I replied honestly.

"Would you like to?" His eyes were fastened on mine.

Would I like to what? I shook my head, trying to clear the cobwebs. I couldn't stop staring at his eyes. They were beautiful, soulful, and intense.

"Would you like to attend my church?" he asked again, apparently oblivious to his effect on people. "If you need a ride, I can even pick you up."

"When?" When had my tongue grown so big and clumsy?

"Tomorrow morning, around ten?"

Suddenly, I found myself staring down at his hands. His nails were clean and trimmed. He wore no wedding band.

"I'm Conner Suthern. I'm a pastor at the church over on First Street."

I wiped my hand on a clean towel and placed it in his. It was warm and smooth, just as I'd suspected that it would be. His fingers closed around mine and squeezed lightly, making me forget for a moment that he was a preacher.

"I'm Rebecca Ward, a bartender at the Meeting Place on Ocean Avenue."

He laughed. "I can see that you've got a sense of humor, Rebecca."

"Yeah, well, you kind of have to have one of those to work here." And, just like that, I was embarrassed about my job, for the first time since I'd started to work at the bar, a year earlier. I didn't know why, either. After all, I made good money—money that allowed me to have a nice apartment, and a decent car.

"So, you'll let me pick you up?" he persisted.

I waited to see if he'd realize what he'd said to me, and how it might have sounded to anyone who'd been listening, but he just kept smiling and staring at me in that wonderful, gentle way—the way that made me feel good about myself.

"Yes," I found myself saying eagerly. "Yes, I'll go to church with you." Or, anywhere else you want me to go, I added silently.

When he beamed, I felt on top of the world. I had made him smile like that. I had made him happy, if only for a few moments. It was a heady, powerful feeling.

Conner picked me up the next morning, and I stayed after the service to help him put together a few baskets of fruit that he planned to take with him when he made his rounds at the hospital. Three of his church members were having surgery, and a fourth was in the last stages of terminal cancer.

A month later, Conner asked me out on a formal date, and that night, as we sat in the park gazing at the stars, I told him my story. I supposed I was frightened that he'd find out all the bad things about me before I could tell him, and I wanted him to hear them from me.

"I quit school and left home when I was sixteen," I began hesitantly. He was an attentive listener and seemed to sense my need to confess everything to him. I figured that he was used to listening to people's troubles.

"I moved in with my boyfriend, Ralph, who sold drugs for a living. We stayed together for a few years. Then, he got busted and went to prison, and I moved in with his best friend." I'd waited to see if he had anything to say about that, but when he'd remained silent, I continued. "Darryl drank, and he had a terrible temper. When he beat me badly one night, I left him. He called the cops and told them that I had stolen a bunch of his stuff."

"Did you?" Conner asked quietly.

"No. The things that I took with me were mine, but I didn't have the sales receipts to prove it. Since it was my first offense, I didn't have to spend any time in jail. They fined me, put me on probation, and gave me community service."

"How old were you?" His eyes were gentle as he looked at me.

"Nineteen." I hesitated then, unsure of whether or not I should continue. In the end, I didn't add that when the police had pulled me over for the stolen items, I'd also been charged with a DUI.

In my mind, I'd rationalized what I'd done by thinking that I wouldn't have been driving at all if Darryl hadn't beaten me. The police, however, hadn't been interested in my bruises, or in the fact that I'd downed a pint of vodka in the hopes of killing the pain. I had no medical insurance, so I didn't go to the emergency room. Besides, I didn't want to answer any questions. Darryl had strong connections, and he didn't mess around when it came to getting even.

When Conner took my hand, I let him. His quiet strength seemed to flow through me, bolstering my courage.

"While I was doing community service, I met this sweet woman named Eloise," I continued. "She offered me a place to stay until I could get on my feet."

"That was nice of her," he commented.

"Yes, it was. Only, her husband wasn't so nice—but she didn't know it." My voice had dropped to a whisper. "He raped me before I could get away from him." I thought that I heard a muffled curse then, but I knew that I had to be mistaken. Conner was a preacher—he wouldn't swear.

"Did you tell her what happened?" He sounded angry and disgusted, but since his hand remained in mine, I knew that his anger and disgust weren't directed toward me.

"No," I admitted, after a reflective moment. "I couldn't do that to her. She thought that the sun rose and set on her husband. Besides, I don't think that he would have believed me."

"She might have," he said.

"I didn't want her to know, okay?" When I realized that I'd snapped at him, I immediately apologized. "I'm sorry. It's just hard for me to tell you these things."

"I understand. So, what did you do next?"

He sounded genuinely interested, so much so that my heart leaped with premature joy. I quickly told myself to be realistic. After all, I knew that Conner wouldn't fall for someone like me—not when there were hundreds of good, decent women out there. He was holding my hand for comfort, and listening so intently because he was a preacher—a man of God.

"I went back home," I told him. "Mom and Dad weren't exactly happy to see me, but they said that I could stay until I found a job and got a place of my own. So, that's what I did."

"And, you've been working at the bar ever since?"

"Oh, no!" I clapped an embarrassed hand over my mouth, then saw that he was smiling. "I worked a dozen jobs before I landed the one that I have. Now, you know all about me. It's your turn."

Conner's life was about as different from mine as it could have been. He told me that he had been raised in a strict, but loving, Christian home along with five siblings—three brothers and two sisters. He had graduated at the top of his class and had gone on to college. It was during college that he received the calling to preach.

I looked down at our entwined hands and thought about his parents. I wondered how they would react to seeing their wonderful son sitting beside a bartender with such a checkered past.

The disapproving images of their faces made me shudder.

72

"Are you cold?" Conner asked solicitously.

I shook my head. How could I explain to him that I felt like a fraud, sitting there next to him? He was all that was good and sweet in the world, and I was everything that was bad and ugly.

Much to my amazement, Conner asked me out on another date, and then, another and another. We dated for eight months, and the entire time, I kept waiting for something terrible to happen. I went to church every Sunday morning and on Sunday evenings, too. I helped Conner with various charities, and sometimes, I went with him on his rounds at the hospital.

Without conscious thought, I began to buy clothes that were more conservative. I donated my old clothes to the needy. I had begun to hope that Conner might want to marry me. But, if I let myself fantasize about it too much, I would panic.

After all, why would Conner want to marry me? I would be an embarrassment to him and to his family, if my past should ever come to light. And, even if no one learned the ugly truth about me, I knew, and Conner knew. I knew that he didn't judge me, but others might.

So, the first time that Conner proposed, I said no. And, believe me, I had to tear that word out of my reluctant throat. Afterward, I cried until I thought that I couldn't cry anymore.

My rejection didn't deter Conner, though. He told me later that he had expected me to say no the first time, and possibly the second time, too. When I asked him why, he smiled.

"Because I know you, Rebecca. You don't realize your own worth. You're a good person, and, someday, I hope that you'll see that."

Everything about Conner made me feel good. His constant praise and sweet words eventually wore me down. That's when I began to consider that maybe, just maybe, I was good enough to be his wife. I began to think that if I worked really hard at it, I could become the kind of woman who was worthy of such a wonderful man.

I knew that if I were given the chance, I would do everything in my power to make him happy. And so, when he proposed the third time, I said yes. Then, I immediately burst into tears. He held me tight and promised me that he would never stop loving me.

The following week, I met Conner's parents. They lived in Missouri, and they'd flown in for the weekend just to meet me. I was a nervous wreck, but with Conner's unwavering patience and praise, I managed to maintain some semblance of calm.

If there had been any alcohol around, I knew that I would have fortified myself with drink or two. I was thankful that I didn't have that opportunity.

Conner's parents were as sweet and as wonderful as he was.

They'd made me feel special and pretty. By the time that they left, my way of thinking about myself had already begun to change. I began to think that maybe it hadn't been a fluke that Conner had seen the good in me. Maybe I actually did have a lot of positive qualities.

I was determined to nourish those good qualities and become someone that I could be proud of. Conner had convinced me that he was already proud of me, and his parents had done the same thing, too. The only one left was the only other person that mattered, and that was me.

A week before our wedding, Conner, with my blessing, had accepted a position as pastor in a small town in Missouri not far from where his parents lived. He told me that he wanted to raise his family in a town where people weren't afraid to leave their doors unlocked.

I agreed, although I was doubtful that such a place really existed in the world anymore. My heart soared, though, at his mention of children. I had always wanted children, and I couldn't wait to hold our first child in my arms. The idea of moving to a small town where nobody knew me was definitely appealing, too.

On our wedding night when Conner took me in his arms, I was already crying.

"I wish that you were the first," I whispered, tracing his beautiful mouth with my finger. "I swear to you before God, Conner, that I will never give you a reason to be ashamed that you married me."

Conner had tears in his eyes, too. He smiled. "When are you going to get it through your head that you could never do anything to make me ashamed that I married you?" he asked.

His passionate words warmed me, yet frightened me at the same time. Could I live up to his expectations, as I had promised?

A month later, we settled into the pretty little parish house that had been provided for us. I was astonished at the fuss that the church members made over us. They even threw me a wedding shower, claiming that I had cheated them out of that pleasure by getting married before we arrived.

Each day that I lived with Conner, I had to pinch myself. I'd been a bartender, and before that, I'd been a nobody who'd bounced from one bad situation to another. Suddenly, I was the wife of a preacher. People respected me, and even admired me. They actually even liked me.

I had to admit, though, that it was not only daunting, but scary. What if my past came to light? It would not only ruin my marriage—it might very well ruin Conner's life. I couldn't stop worrying about it. I supposed I was afraid to be happy.

Conner knew that I worried, and he did his best to reassure me that everything was going to be just fine. We were in God's hands, he told me, and God loved us.

I learned how to pray for the first time in my life, and each time

I prayed, I asked God to guide me and to give me the wisdom and the strength to remain on the right path. I thanked Him several times a day for giving me Conner—and another chance at life.

The church where Conner was the pastor was a small, quaint church with a dedicated, loyal congregation. Everyone seemed happy and content with Conner as their pastor. Conner, in return, thrived on small-town life. He coached the Little League team, taught Sunday school, and organized a vacation Bible school for the children. Together, we were very involved with local charities.

Eventually, the determined women of that small town began to draw me into their circle. I was happy, but still painfully shy, when it came to public speaking—or, when I found myself the center of attention, as I inevitably did. The way that the women vied for my attention and tried to impress me not only embarrassed me—it reminded me that I wasn't the person whom they believed that I was. I didn't feel worthy of their attention and praise.

But, again, they were a determined bunch of women. When I made excuses not to get involved, they removed the excuses with a tenacity that I couldn't help but admire. Within weeks, I was so busy that I didn't have much time to think about my past.

Not everyone liked me, of course. Phoebe Warren was a prime example. She clucked and fussed and praised me as much as anyone, and yet, I knew, in my heart, that she wasn't sincere. Sometimes, I'd caught her watching me through narrowed eyes—as if she somehow knew that I wasn't fit to be a preacher's wife and was looking for a way to expose me.

Then there was her friends, Marilyn and Laura. When those three were together, the conversation usually got personal. They asked questions that I had to avoid—or lie about. Since I preferred not to lie, I usually answered vaguely, or changed the subject.

"Do you see your parents often, Rebecca?" Marilyn asked during a church meeting one day. We had all gathered at my house to decide how we were going to raise money and food for the families who were in need during the Christmas holidays. We all had pencils and paper before us so that we could jot down our ideas for a fund raiser, then pool the ideas together.

With my head down, I tapped my pencil on the pad, aware that everyone had gone quiet at Marilyn's question. I would have bet the following Sunday's offerings that Phoebe Warren had put Marilyn up to asking the question.

That question, I could, at least, answer honestly. But, I knew that there would be more question, questions that I wouldn't—or couldn't—answer, not unless I found some way to change the subject without looking obvious.

75

"No, I don't, Marilyn. Both my parents still work and aren't home much," I answered. That was the truth, too. My dad was an electrician, and my mother worked in a bank.

"How about your brothers and sisters? Do you keep in touch?" Marilyn was still asking the questions, and everyone else was quiet and listening.

I scribbled something on the paper, hoping to appear casual. I knew that I couldn't tell those God-fearing churchwomen to mind their own business, but I wanted to.

"I only have one brother, and he joined the Marines before I left home," I told her.

"Left home? You mean, to get married to Pastor Suthern?" she persisted

Slowly, I set down the pencil. In a short amount of time, Marilyn had backed me into a corner. I had to bite my tongue to keep from telling her the truth—every ugly word of it—just to get it over and done with. It was the thought of Conner that stopped me.

"Like a lot of misguided teenagers, I left home when I was very young—long before I met my husband. I don't really like to talk about those years in between," I said firmly.

I'd known that I was taking a chance on alienating the woman, and had probably increased everyone else's curiosity, but I hadn't known what else to say.

"Marilyn, we all have things in our lives that we'd rather not talk about. Leave it alone."

Surprisingly, Laura had come to my rescue. I silently thanked her with my eyes, and she winked at me, as if we were best friends.

Could I have been wrong about Laura? I wondered.

Marilyn sniffed, sounding offended by Laura's reprimand. "Well, we're all one, happy family, aren't we? Besides, it's our money that pays her husband's salary, so I think that we have the right to know—" she began.

She broke off as I stood up, knocking my pencil to the floor. I knew that my face was red—I could feel the heat of it.

"I'm not a serial killer," I said softly. "I'm not a child molester, and I've never been a prostitute. Have I covered everything, Marilyn? And, while we're being honest here, have I done something to make you doubt me?"

Marilyn had turned two shades lighter at the beginning of my outburst. Suddenly, twin spots of color splashed her cheeks.

"I'm sorry, Rebecca. I didn't mean to upset you. No, you haven't done anything to make me doubt that you're a good, Christian woman."

It was on the tip of my tongue to blurt out to those good women that I hadn't always led a Christian life, but I didn't. Conner would be disturbed enough by that little incident without my making it worse.

To my surprise, Conner laughed when I told him, later that evening, what had happened. I stared at him in shock.

"You're not angry?" I asked.

"Angry?" He pulled me close, his hands caressing my body. "I'm proud of the way that you handled it. I couldn't have done it better myself."

For a pastor, Conner could be extremely naughty when it came to making love to his wife. Sometimes, he even shocked me, and that wasn't easy to do. I guess it was because I had expected a preacher to be more—well, conservative in bed. When I shyly told him that, he laughed and proceeded to shock me further by hoisting me to the kitchen counter and making love to me right there in broad daylight.

"God is love and joy, Rebecca," he told me afterward, in a breathless, sated voice. "Don't you think he rejoices when he sees two people who love each other making love?" His sudden grin was boyish and endearing. "Besides, I can't help myself around you, and preachers are human, too."

I shook my head, coming out of my daydream just in time to catch the last of Conner's words.

"They had no right to pry into our personal lives, anyway," he said. "Paying my salary doesn't give them that right."

Perversely, I found myself defending the women. "It's human nature to be curious about someone," I said.

"As long as you don't let your curiosity hurt that someone, then there's nothing wrong with it," he told me.

As usual, Conner's wise words made sense. I became distracted as Conner started to unfasten my blouse.

"Eventually," he said between kisses, "they'll love you so much that they'll forget about their curiosity."

The next day, I got the shock of my life, but it was nothing compared to what happened afterward. . . .

I had stopped at the supermarket to pick up a few things for supper. I'd found a new recipe, and I couldn't wait to try it. Humming to myself, I was watching the pavement instead of where I was going, so I didn't see the man until I reached my car.

"Hey, Rebecca. Long time no see," he said.

A hum lodged in my throat, then died a quick death as I looked up to find my ex-boyfriend, Ralph, leaning against a muddy car that was parked next to my own.

My arm tightened instinctively around my grocery bag. I looked quickly around to see if anyone was watching.

"Ralph. When did you get out of prison again?" Before I'd met

Conner, I'd heard through the grapevine that he'd gotten out, and that a few months later, he'd gotten caught stealing a car.

Before he could answer, I thought of another, more important question: "How did you find me?" I asked apprehensively.

He folded his arms over his chest, cocking his head to stare at me. For the first time, I noticed that he really looked like an ex-con—tough and mean.

"Your mom told me." He shrugged, eyeing my nice, modest dress. "You've changed."

"I'm married," I said quickly, taking a step in the direction of my car and hoping that he'd take the hint. "I'm married to a preacher," I added for good measure.

His disbelieving laughter scalded my ears. When he saw that I wasn't laughing with him, he smirked. "You really did marry a preacher! Well, isn't that a shock. You, of all people, married to a preacher. Does he know that I was your first?"

I hadn't heard that kind of crude talk in a long time, and I certainly hadn't missed it. Battling humiliating tears, I opened my car door and threw the bag of groceries onto the passenger seat. I turned back around and gave Ralph a cold look.

"Leave me alone, Ralph," I told him.

He acted as if I hadn't spoken, jerking his head in the direction of the church steeple that was visible in the distance.

"Is that where your little hubby preaches?" he taunted. "I just might have to stick around and go to church so that I can meet him."

That time, I couldn't stop the tears. "Don't, Ralph," I begged shamelessly. "If you ever cared about me, you'll leave this town right now and forget that you ever saw me."

As I drove away, I could still hear his jeering laughter ringing in my ears. My tears nearly blinded me. Finally, I pulled to the side of the road and slammed on my brakes, spilling the sack of groceries onto the floor. I sat there, crying helplessly, scared to death that Ralph was about to ruin my life.

After a while, I picked up the groceries and put them back into the bag. I sat there for a moment, holding the bottle of cooking wine that I'd bought, and thinking about my impending conversation with Conner. I knew that I would have to tell him about meeting Ralph in town so that he could be prepared. Maybe Conner would know what to do.

Just one drink to calm my nerves, I thought, unscrewing the cap. I tilted the cooking wine to my mouth and took two or three good swallows. It tasted awful, but the result was almost immediate. I felt calmer right away. I capped the bottle and stuck it back into the bag. Then, I said a quick prayer, asking for forgiveness. I checked for traffic, then pulled back onto the road.

The church was about a mile out of town, and the parish where we lived another was a little further along the same shady, tree-lined road. I drove slowly to give myself time to think.

Together, Conner and I could figure out how to handle Ralph if he made good on his promise and came to church. Perhaps, Conner could turn Ralph's life around, as he had helped to turn mine around. Conner had that special, God-given talent.

As I drew closer to home, I made an effort to wipe the tears from my face, using the back of my sleeve. I had taken my eyes from the road for just a second, and when I looked again, there was a child on a bicycle directly in my path.

I screamed and hit my brakes, but it was too late. There was a heavy thud, the screech of metal on pavement as the bicycle caught on the undercarriage of my car, and the sound of my brakes working overtime.

Then, there was silence. An awful silence—the kind that makes you wish for any sound at all.

I sat there for possibly thirty seconds, horrified by what had happened, trying to get my dazed mind around the facts. My hands were shaking as I rolled the window down and looked out.

Maybe it wasn't a child, I thought hopefully. Maybe it was just something in the road and I just imagined that it was a child. Please God, I prayed, don't let it be a child.

But God, apparently, wasn't listening.

The child lay sprawled on the road to my left, lying on his stomach with one arm twisted at an unnatural angle against his side. A backpack lay beside him—his things had been scattered onto the road.

"Oh, no," I whispered, covering my mouth to keep the screams inside. "Oh, dear God, please let him be all right!"

I don't know why I moved my car, but I did. I backed it up until I could see the bicycle again. Then, I pulled my car to the side of the road and had the presence of mind to put on the flashers before I got out.

When I tried to stand up, I had to grab the door for support. My legs buckled again and again, and it took several attempts before I could walk to where the boy lay. I didn't think that my heart had ever pounded so hard before. It hurt, just as my throat hurt as I fought to keep from screaming like a madwoman.

I fell to my knees beside the boy, afraid to touch him, and afraid to roll him over for fear of what I'd find. Vaguely, I heard a car in the background, over the roaring that was growing louder and louder in my ears.

I heard the sounds of breaks screeching, and then the sound of footsteps running toward me.

"Are you all right?" a man's worried voice asked me. "Do you know what happened? Mrs. Suthern? I'm Bud, from the station. Can you hear me?"

I heard him, but I couldn't answer. I couldn't take my eyes from that still little figure lying in the road.

I had done the unspeakable: I had hit that little boy with my car.

"Was it a hit-and-run accident?" the man asked me again. "Did you see the car? You wait right here. I'll get the ambulance and the sheriff. Probably some drunk driver!"

It figured that our little town would have a sheriff, instead of a modern police chief. I knew that I must have been in shock to have been thinking the things that I had. Why else would I have thought those things while a little boy lay broken on the road—possibly dead?

Hit-and-run.

The words sliced through my mind like a shark through water—silent and deadly.

Bud, from the gas station, had just assumed that someone else had plowed into the boy on his bicycle, and that I had merely happened along. Possibly, he'd thought that because I had moved my car to the side of the road.

When they found out that it was me, they'd check my driving history and find out that I had once been charged with DUI, and that I'd had a felony. Being the preacher's wife wouldn't stop the sheriff from doing his duty—and the sheriff and his wife were members of our congregation.

I knew that they'd find the opened bottle of cooking wine in the car, and although I knew that I hadn't had enough to have impaired my driving, they would wonder and whisper—and draw their own conclusions.

And, if Ralph came to church, as I'd suspected he would, then he would give them more food for gossip, so they would have even more reason to believe the worst about me.

The people in town would be shocked and disappointed. They might ask for Conner's resignation.

Conner loved the town, and he loved his church. He loved the people, and they loved him. They'd merely tolerated me because of Conner. At least, those were the thoughts that went through my shocked mind at the time.

I wasn't sure how long I knelt in the road before Bud returned with the sheriff. It couldn't have been long, though.

In the distance, I heard a siren wailing and knew that the ambulance was on its way.

The sheriff's concerned, grim face came into view as he knelt on the other side of the boy. His voice was soft and gentle, as if he knew that I wasn't far from breaking down.

"Mrs. Suthern, I need to know. Did you see the vehicle?" he asked.

A hit-and-run, I thought. Even the sheriff believed it. He hadn't even considered the possibility that it had been me.

I had an instant to make one of the most important decisions of my life. "I think she might be in shock, sheriff. Somebody ought to find Pastor Suthern."

It was Bud again, saving me from having to answer. He couldn't have known that he was working for the devil.

I felt strong arms lift me to my feet and hold me steady. The ambulance had arrived. The EMTs were racing in our direction.

"We need to stand back, Mrs. Suthern," the sheriff said gently.

"Yes." I had spoken, but the sound was so faint that I doubted that anyone had heard me. He led me to my car.

"I think that you should sit down," he advised.

"Yes." It was all I could seem to say. I sat in the driver's seat with my legs out of the car and my arm resting on the steering wheel. My head felt funny. I was close to fainting.

Was the child dead? Had I killed him?

The sheriff knelt down beside me. "Mrs. Suthern, I know that you're in shock, but I need for you to tell me if you saw the vehicle," he said softly. "The sooner I go after him, the sooner I can throw him in jail."

Through the fog of shock, I realized that the sheriff assumed that it was a man who'd hit the boy, not a woman. That was his second wrong assumption. For a hysterical moment, I envisioned blurting out the truth, and the sheriff not believing me. I was the preacher's wife—incapable of committing such a terrible deed.

The irony was not lost on me.

I licked my dry lips, then tried to swallow before I said the damning words.

"I—I didn't see the vehicle," I whispered.

The sheriff sighed as if he weren't surprised. "I was afraid of that. So, he was already lying in the road when you reached him," he said.

It wasn't a question, so I didn't answer.

"How could anyone not see a child on a bicycle?" He rubbed his chin and sighed again, as if he were disgusted with the world in general. "The driver just left the scene of the crime. He probably had something to hide."

I finally realized that the sheriff wasn't talking to me, but more to himself. But, his words cut through me, anyway. He was right. The person who had hit the boy definitely had something to hide—many, many things to hide.

His next comment struck terror into my heart, and I was immediately ashamed.

"Maybe the boy will be all right, and he can identify the vehicle."

The boy had to be all right. If he wasn't, then I had killed him. Yet, if he identified my car, then I would lose everything. I would lose Conner. And, I'd lose the respect that I craved. I'd lose the home that I loved. Even more important, I'd lose the babies that I would never have with Conner.

We were talking about my life, and I was desperately afraid of losing it. At the cost of my integrity, at the cost of my soul, I was protecting it by lying.

What harm am I doing by lying? I thought. Either the boy would be all right or he wouldn't. Hitting him had been an accident—an honest accident. If I were the type of person that they all believed I was, I could have told them the truth—that it had been an innocent accident—and they would have believed me.

But, the truth was, I wasn't that person. I was a fraud. A fake. I was an ex-bartender with a record. I had taken a few drinks out of a bottle of cooking wine just before the accident, because I had met someone in town—someone who held the power to destroy me.

"Rebecca?"

At the sound of Conner's voice, I looked up. He stood there in front of me, his sweet, wonderful face full of concern.

My pain and fear fell away for the moment as I rose and stumbled into his loving arms.

This is the reason that I lied, I thought, sobbing onto Conner's shoulder. I didn't think that I could have gone on living without Conner.

"Shh, baby. I think he's going to be all right. The paramedics are taking him to the hospital right now. We'll follow, okay? And, we'll stay with him until we find out if he's going to make it."

Gently, as if I were a piece of valuable china and Conner feared that I'd break, he led me around to the passenger side of the car. When he opened the door and leaned in, I realized that he was putting the spilled groceries back into the bag, unaware that it was the second time that they'd been spilled.

He paused for a moment. I stiffened and forgot to breathe. Had he found the cooking wine? Was he puzzling over the amount that was missing? Would he figure out what had really happened?

But no, he had been merely transferring the bag over the seat into the back. Then, he helped me inside, buckling my seat belt as if I was a child.

The ambulance headed back to town. The nearest hospital was located about fifteen miles away. Conner started my car and headed after the ambulance.

Once again, I held my breath. I had run over the bicycle. What if I'd damaged something underneath the car? What if I'd ripped a hole in the oil pan? Conner would know that I'd hit something, and without much effort, he would put two and two together.

A wave of nausea hit me as the full realization of what I'd done sank in. I had sealed my fate with those damning words. Now, I was doomed, either way. If I came forward and confessed, the sheriff would ask me why I hadn't told the truth in the first place. I'd have to explain to him. But, if I didn't come forward, I would have to live with the awful deception for the rest of my life.

Unless, of course, the boy was only moderately injured. Surely, God would forgive me then? Surely, I could forgive myself?

The ride to the hospital seemed interminable. The sheriff had obviously contacted the boy's parents, because they were waiting when we arrived at the hospital, along with a little girl. I recognized them immediately as members of our church, although I hadn't had time to get to know them personally.

Nancy and Evan Potter looked dazed. Nancy's eyes were swollen, so I knew that she'd been crying. As Conner led me inside to the emergency waiting room and to a chair, I recalled that the Potters had two children, Lisa and Brandon. So, it must have been Brandon that I had hit.

I watched, mired in guilt and fear, as Conner soothed and comforted the Potters. They all bowed their heads in prayer, and I did the same. My prayer was simple, but fervent: Please, God, let him be all right, I prayed. Forgive me, dear Lord, for my deception. I was frightened and I lost my way.

It was a shameful prayer, considering that I had come to my senses and still hadn't told anyone the truth.

Conner returned to me after a time and put his arm around my shoulders. He drew me against his chest. I went willingly, and the tears came again. He tilted my face and stared into my eyes.

"If you've ever needed proof of the goodness inside you, Rebecca, you've got it now. You don't even know this child, yet your heart is breaking."

His loving words spilled like acid onto my heart. I wasn't worthy of that man. I wasn't worthy of those wonderful people surrounding us.

But the words that would both set me free and condemn me just wouldn't come. I could only cry and hate myself. At the moment, I couldn't stand the thought of losing Conner, even though I knew that I didn't deserve him.

As time went by, other members of the congregation crowded into the small waiting room. The news had traveled, and people stood around in groups and talked in low voices, while others prayed. The worst part had come when they'd learned that I had been the one to find him.

One by one, they'd come to me and offered comfort through hugs or prayer. Each time they touched me, I felt the flames of hell lick higher and higher. I could almost feel my feet burning.

"I can imagine how finding him must have shaken you," one elderly woman said, clucking her head in sympathy. "How anyone could hit a child like that and just leave him to die?"

But, I didn't leave him to die! I wanted to shout. I just hadn't admitted that I was the one they'd spoken of with such disgust and disbelief.

Conner nudged me out of my stupor. "The doctor said that he's going to make it, but he's still unconscious. He has a broken leg, a concussion, and some other injuries."

Silently, I stared at him. I should tell him now, I thought. I should just stand up and tell the truth.

"Let's go in and pray, shall we?" Conner pulled me to my feet and put his arm around my waist for support. The crowd parted as we made our way to the temporary room where they'd placed Brandon, until a room upstairs could be prepared.

I couldn't stop a gasp when I saw him. He looked so helpless and small, and so very, very pale against the whiteness of the bed sheets.

His leg was in a temporary cast until a bone specialist could take over. The bandage around his head covered most of his hair, and there was an ugly bruise on his face that looked as if it would be there for a long time to come.

Conner held my hand as we prayed for Brandon's speedy recovery, and thanked God for sparing his life. My knees nearly buckled when Conner prayed for the lost soul of the person who was responsible for injuring the child.

Was God listening? Would he answer Conner's prayers and forgive me? I was terribly afraid that he wouldn't—at least, not while I remained silent.

Since Brandon was out of the woods, Conner and I went home. There were still uniformed policemen milling around the area of the accident. The sheriff hailed him, and Conner stopped the car and rolled down his window.

"Find anything?" he asked.

The sheriff looked grim as he came closer to the window and looked inside. His gaze touched briefly on me before he focused on Conner.

"It looks like whoever hit him dragged that bike a few feet. We'd probably find some paint from the bike on the undercarriage—if we knew who to look for."

My heart stopped when the sheriff looked at me again. "Someone said that there was a stranger in town earlier, driving a muddy car. You didn't happen to notice him, did you, Mrs. Suthern?" he asked.

My mouth went dry. Had someone seen me talking to Ralph? Was the sheriff testing me? Or, was he merely asking, just as he might ask anyone?

Once again, I didn't know what to say. If I told him that yes, I had noticed the muddy car, then the sheriff would question Ralph. Ralph would likely use the opportunity to talk about me to the sheriff. If I said no, that I hadn't seen the car, then I would be lying.

Yes, I know that I'd lied already, but I didn't want to keep heaping sin upon sin—not if I could avoid it.

But, Ralph might also mention my past record, which might make the sheriff suspicious.

"No, I didn't. I'm sorry," I murmured.

"No need to be sorry, ma'am." The sheriff tipped his hat and waved us on. "See you on Sunday!"

When we got home, I made it a point of putting the groceries away before Conner saw the opened bottle of cooking wine. Then I pleaded a headache—which wasn't a lie—and went to lie down. Conner said he'd start our dinner and check on me later.

I never went to sleep, of course. There was no chance of that, not with a dozen questions whirling inside my head.

What if Brandon had seen my car or recognized me through the windshield before I'd hit him?

What if Ralph came to church on Sunday, like he'd threatened to do?

What if the sheriff began checking under every car that had been spotted in the area that day? Logically, he would start with my car. What if he did he would find the scratches on the undercarriage, and, possibly, the paint.

Finally, my mind got around to asking myself when I was planning on talking to Conner about seeing Ralph. When would we discuss the possible threat he posed to our peaceful existence?

I closed my eyes and moaned, wondering why it seemed as though God had suddenly deserted me. Was what I was going through my punishment for everything that I'd done that was bad in my life? To be given a wonderful husband and a respectable, happy life for a few months—then, to have it yanked away from me?

"Rebecca? Are you feeling better, honey?"

I opened my eyes to find Conner standing by the bed, holding a tray in his hands. He'd brought my food to me.

It was too much. I threw the covers aside and got out of bed, forcing him to step quickly out of my way. My voice was ugly then, and the tone was one that I'd never used with him before.

"Stop being so nice to me! I don't deserve it!" I snapped.

"Rebecca—" he began.

I turned on him. Guilt, pain, and fear had made me reckless. "No, don't say it. Don't say anything about how good and wonderful I am. Because, you see, I'm not. Do you understand, Conner? I'm not a good person. I never have been. You just convinced yourself that I was, and I went along with it."

Conner actually smiled at me. "You're in shock, Rebecca. You don't know what you're saying," he told me.

"I saw Ralph today in town," I blurted out.

"Ralph?" Conner's smile faded. "Your old boyfriend?"

"Yes." Tears threatened, but I didn't feel I deserved the luxury. "He was driving a muddy car."

Conner looked shocked. "But, if you knew this, why didn't you tell the sheriff?" he asked slowly.

"Because I was afraid." My voice dropped to a whisper. I felt the tears slipping down my cheeks. "Because I was afraid! If the sheriff went looking for Ralph and found him, I was afraid of what Ralph would say about me. He'd already threatened to come to church to meet you."

"I'll welcome him with open arms, honey." Conner spoke in a soothing, gentle voice, but for once, it didn't work its usual magic. It irritated me instead.

"You don't understand!" I shouted, startling him. "It's not your past that he'll be digging up for everyone to examine."

"But, Rebecca, if he really hit Brandon—" Conner began again.

"He couldn't have." I shook my head vehemently. "I spoke to him right before I found Brandon, so it couldn't have been him. He would have had to pass me, and he didn't."

Tell him now! my conscience urged. But, I couldn't do it. I just simply could not tell my husband what I'd done—that I was the monster who'd hit that little boy. Brandon was going to be all right. He would heal. Those were the words that I kept repeating to myself. If Brandon had died, I didn't think that I could have stood the guilt, but he hadn't died.

The phone rang, interrupting our heated exchange. Conner set the tray on the bed and answered it.

"Hello? Oh, thank God!" He turned to face me, grinning happily. "Brandon is conscious!"

I forced a smile to my lips. "That's wonderful," I whispered.

Conner returned his attention to the voice on the other end, asking the question that had kept me paralyzed with fear: "Has he said anything? Did he see who hit him?"

When Conner's smile faded abruptly, my heart almost stopped.

"Brandon said he didn't see who it was," he told me. "He doesn't even remember what happened."

I sat on the edge of the bed before my legs betrayed me. Brandon couldn't identify me. I was safe.

But, there was still Ralph to deal with. And after Ralph, then what? Another ghost from my past? Should I keep lying and hiding the truth for fear of what those people will think of me? Was that how I wanted to live my life?

Conner sat beside me and took my cold hands in his. He squeezed them. "Rebecca, you have to have faith in people. I love the person that you are now, and they love the person that you are now. The rest doesn't matter."

I didn't know why, but I couldn't let myself believe Conner. I knew that he was smart and good, but his goodness was what made me doubt that he knew what he was talking about. He believed everyone was good—therefore, they were.

It didn't work that way, though, and I knew it. There were bad people in the world—many more of them than Conner could imagine.

Just then, I felt that he was married to one of them.

"Marrying me was a mistake," I said.

He looked at me in shock for a moment. Then, he burst out laughing. He pulled me against his chest and held me so tightly that I couldn't breathe.

"You are one in a million, do you know that? God must really love me to let me have you for a wife. I love you, Rebecca," he told me.

Trying to convince Conner of something that he wasn't capable of believing was frustrating, to say the least. I let out a shuddering sigh and inhaled the rich, clean scent of my husband. His arms were strong and loving, and his lips on my forehead were both soothing and arousing. I kissed his neck and I heard a sound of pleasure in his throat.

I wanted to make love. I wanted Conner to show me how much he loved me. I wanted him to prove to me that, no matter what happened, he would never stop loving me.

He lowered me onto the bed and undressed me, then stood to take off his own clothes and to move the dinner tray to a safer place. When he joined me again, I felt the earth move beneath us. Each time we made love, I felt such a rich, wonderful feeling of acceptance and peace—something that I'd never experienced with any other man.

That time was no exception, and I took that as a good sign. Maybe God had understood my reasons for lying, and was showing His approval.

I soon found out that I had been only kidding myself.

Ralph did show up for the Sunday service, taking a seat in the back pew. I felt his eyes on me, and I knew that he was there even before I turned around and saw him.

His smile looked threatening and evil.

I tried to concentrate on the sermon that my husband was giving with such enthusiasm and passion, but I found my mind wandering back to the past.

Ralph had been the bad boy that all the girls had loved to giggle and fantasize over. He'd graduated the year before, but still, he'd driven his sister to school on his motorcycle and had hung around to talk to the older boys. I'd suspected even then that he had been selling drugs. The possibility should have turned me off, but, instead, I'd found the thrill of danger a lure that I couldn't resist.

One day, I had been walking home from school with two of my friends. Ralph had come roaring by on his bike, and I'd automatically lifted a hand to wave at him. Being painfully shy, I had been immediately mortified by my actions.

My friends had thought that I had lost my mind. It was nothing, though, compared to what they thought when I'd gotten on the back of that motorcycle with Ralph and taken off.

Even years later, I couldn't explain what had come over me. I hadn't said a word when Ralph had turned his bike around and come back, idling alongside of us. I'd offered him a shy smile, and he'd offered me a ride.

We had been inseparable after that. I'd quit school and moved in with Ralph, and I'd gotten a job working at the local diner. If Ralph hadn't gotten busted, I might have even still been with him.

I shivered at the thought, and the lady next to me offered me her sweater. I smiled and shook my head. For a moment, my gaze connected with my husband's, and in that second, I knew that he had spotted Ralph and realized who he was.

His look both reassured and comforted me. I knew then that I wasn't alone anymore. I had Conner, and he was my husband. He'd pledged to protect and love me—till death do us part.

We sang hymns and Conner, in that soft, deep voice of his, invited the sinners to come forward and take Jesus into their hearts. Finally, the service ended with a heartfelt prayer.

Then, it was a time for fellowship as everyone moved slowly to the double doors of the church. Outside, the weather was warm and sunny—a beautiful day.

The moment I stepped outside, Ralph approached me. He was dressed in a suit and a tie. I'd never seen him in anything but leather and jeans, so I was understandably surprised.

"Your husband has talent. He almost convinced me that I was worth saving," he said, with that shark smile that made me want to run away, screaming. He laughed, but I didn't laugh with him.

"You are worth saving, Ralph. Everyone is," I told him. Except maybe me, I thought darkly.

"Who's your friend, Rebecca?"

I stiffened at the sound of Phoebe Warren's strident, artificial voice and searched desperately for Conner. I spotted him at the door.

"Um, this is an old high school friend of mine, Ralph Russo. Ralph, meet Phoebe Warren."

Ralph's laugh turned my blood into ice. "Now, Rebecca, we were much more than friends," he drawled, watching my face. "We lived together."

Phoebe gasped. I turned at least two shades of red. If I hadn't spotted Conner striding our way, I might have lost my dignity and began trying to scratch out Ralph's evil eyes. Why was he doing such a thing to me? Just because he could? Or, was it my punishment for having kept my terrible secret?

"I'm sorry, Rebecca," Ralph sneered. "Did I embarrass you in front of your church friend?"

Just then, Conner put his arm around my waist. "You must be Ralph," he said, without a trace of anger. "I know all about you, and I don't appreciate your making vulgar remarks about my wife. So, I think that you should leave, unless you want to go back inside and pray with me."

Ralph looked taken aback. I was sure that he hadn't expected Ralph to defend me, or to order him to leave.

"Do you know what kind of woman you married, man?" he asked.

"I married a wonderful, loving, generous-hearted woman who doesn't deserve to have her character sullied." Conner spoke with confidence and pride.

Others, drawn by the tension, had gathered around us. They remained silent, listening. I couldn't tell what they were thinking, but I'd assumed the worst.

"You don't know her, preacher man," Ralph said.

"She's my wife. Of course, I know her. We hide nothing from each other. Now, I suggest that you leave before I forget that I'm a preacher," he ordered.

It amazed me, the way that Conner could speak without portraying any anger or hatred. I knew, without a doubt, that if Ralph had suddenly asked for Conner's help, Conner would have gone to his knees to pray for Ralph right there on the grass in the churchyard.

Was it any wonder that I loved that man?

I pulled at Conner's sleeve. "Let's go, Conner. I think that we're finished here."

"We'll pray for you, Ralph," Conner said sincerely. "Come back to church anytime."

We left Ralph standing there with Phoebe Warren—whom, I had no doubt, couldn't wait to fill everyone in on what they had missed. At the moment, I was too weary and filled with guilt to care.

Conner had proudly exclaimed that he and I had hid nothing from each other. But, he was wrong. I was hiding a terrible secret from him—and the entire town—and it was eating at my soul. As long as I harbored that dark lie, I knew that I was no better than Ralph.

I was unusually silent for the rest of the day, and again at church that night. Conner kept casting me worried looks, but I figured that he just assumed I was embarrassed about the encounter with Ralph.

My guilt increased when I realized that not one soul in the congregation had looked at me with anything but loving acceptance. Phoebe Warren was curiously absent, but her husband was there, sitting a few rows back from where I sat and looking oddly smug about something. Whenever our eyes met, he smiled and nodded, leaving me more baffled than ever.

Later, I learned that he had forbid Phoebe to come to church until she could stop gossiping about me and until she could treat me with the respect that I deserved.

When our choir leader began singing, I couldn't keep the tears at bay any longer. I was falling apart inside. Without the structure of my faith, I was left with an unsteady foundation, and it was collapsing around me.

Before I lost my courage, I left the aisle and approached Conner, who'd kept his head bowed as he sang—waiting for the lost sinners to come forward.

I knew that I'd never forget the shock on his face when he'd realized that I had come forward. But, he took my hands and bent his head to listen to my plea for help, just as he would have done for anyone.

"I need to speak to the congregation," I whispered to my husband.

Conner nodded and lifted his arms to halt the music. When everyone was silent, he continued.

"My wife needs to speak with you, brothers and sisters. Afterward, we'll continue our benediction. I urge anyone who carries a burden to come forward and seek renewal from Jesus Christ, our Lord and Savior. Not a single soul in this building is without sin. Not a single soul, including myself, could cast the first stone. We're all human. God knows this and loves us, anyway," he said.

On trembling legs, I made my way to the pulpit and faced the congregation. My gaze sought the Potter family sitting about halfway back with their two children. Brandon still wore a bandage on his head, and a cast on his leg, but he seemed fine.

Nancy Potter smiled at me, and I nearly burst into sobs right then and there.

What I was about to do would be one of the hardest things that I'd ever done in my life. And it wasn't just getting up before a few hundred people, either. No, it was having to say what I needed to say.

People began to stir restlessly before I finally began to speak. I kept my gaze on the Bible that was spread open on the pulpit.

"When I met Conner, I was a bartender." I paused, mildly surprised when I heard only a few murmurs of surprise. "He walked into the bar where I worked to leave a stack of inspirational brochures, and asked me to go to church with him. I accepted. We began to date, and, eventually, Conner asked me to marry him." I looked up for a brief moment and smiled through my tears. I wanted everyone to know how happy that memory was for me. "I said no."

The crowd shifted and murmured their disbelief, then grew quiet again.

"Conner, as some of you might know, can be stubborn." I got a few chuckles out of that one. "He continued to ask me, until I agreed to marry him. You see, I never thought that I was good enough for Conner. He convinced me that I was." I paused.

"We moved to this town soon after we were married. I lived in fear, at first, that someone would find out about my past and judge me. Well, you all did find out, and you didn't judge me." I used the edge of my sleeve to wipe the tears from my eyes. "That's why I have to tell you the truth about what happened on the day that Brandon got hit."

There were murmurs of shock throughout the church. When I chanced a glance at the Potters, they were frowning.

I forced myself to continue. "A few of you met Ralph, my ex-boyfriend. Well, I saw him in town that day. My parents had told him where to find me. He'd threatened to tell everyone what a bad person I had once been. I'll admit that I was worried that his plan would succeed." My voice was trembling.

"On the way home, I was crying and shaking so badly that I had to pull over to the side of the road. I took a few drinks of the cooking wine that I had purchased at the store to calm my nerves. Finally, I got back onto the road. That's when I hit Brandon."

That time, the murmuring of the crowd rose to a dull roar. Conner, who had been watching me from the front row, came to stand beside me. He lifted his hand to quiet the congregation.

I ignored him, knowing that I had to do it on my own.

"The only excuse I have was that I didn't see him. One moment, I was wiping my tears away with my sleeve, and the next he was just—just there." At that point, I didn't dare to look at anyone. "I backed up and pulled my car to the side of the road, so when Bud arrived, he just assumed that I had found Brandon. The sheriff assumed the same thing. I allowed them to believe it, and I allowed them to believe it because I was afraid. I not only have a felony charge on my past record, but I also have a driving-while-intoxicated charge. That's not the person who I am now, but I was afraid that you all would think the worst of me."

Tears slipped from my chin and fell onto the open Bible. I stared straight ahead. "I'm asking for your forgiveness. I should have trusted you with the truth. I should have trusted God—and myself," I concluded.

To my amazement and joy, the congregation stood as one. Then, they began to filter into the aisle and head in my direction. The Potter family took the lead. Many had tears in their eyes. A few wept openly. They gathered around me, surrounding me with their warmth, their faith—and their acceptance.

My husband smiled down at me through his own tears, conveying a timeless love that I could never take for granted.

I was truly blessed. Even now, I sometimes think about how close I came to losing everything, and I shudder. No charges were filed, and the accident was deemed just that—an accident.

Then, I get down on my knees and thank God for His wisdom.

THE END

STALKED FROM
THE GRAVE
Who is trying to hurt me?

A mysterious voice asked: "Good morning, sunshine. How are you today?"

My palms had started sweating. "Who is this? Why are you doing this to me?" I screamed into the phone.

"Sunshine, what am I doing? I'm just calling you to say hello. What's the matter?"

My blood had run cold as I'd dropped the phone. My husband ran over to me and grabbed me by the waist. He'd taken the phone and greeted the caller. Apparently, the person wasn't responding to him, because he'd kept repeating himself over and over again. Finally, he'd hung up.

"Honey, what happened?" he asked, helping me to a nearby chair.

"I don't know. The caller asked me how I was doing and called me by the same nickname that my grandmother used to call me." I knew that I'd sounded crazy when I'd seen the expression on my husband's face. He was looking at me as if I had grown two heads.

"Honey, you have to get some counseling. This is getting to be too much. Anyone could have that nickname—it's not uncommon. You miss your grandma so much that you're really starting to worry me."

I couldn't believe that my husband was talking to me like some child—a child who had just told him a story about monsters in the closet. How dare he insult my intelligence like that?

"I know what I heard!" I insisted, jumping up from my chair.

"Honey, calm down," he told me. "Let's discuss this later."

"I don't want to discuss anything later. Just leave me alone!" I yelled, sitting on the couch. Cliff had walked into the kitchen, leaving me alone with my thoughts.

After that, I'd gone into Grandma's room and just looked around. Although Grandma had been in her early eighties, she'd loved perfume. She wouldn't walk out of the house without putting some behind her ears. I'd picked up a bottle to smell the scent.

Returning the perfume to her dresser, I'd looked through her drawers. Everything was folded so neatly—just the way she'd liked it. Her socks and stockings were balled into neat little piles, and she'd even color-coordinated them. I'd smiled to myself, remembering when she'd told me that neatness was a sign of sanity. My grandmother always had been very sane, so I supposed that there was some kind of truth in her words.

Probing further into her drawers, I'd noticed for the first time what beautiful sweaters and blouses she'd had. Then, putting back her sweaters, I'd noticed the drawer underneath, which was full of knickknacks. Rummaging through her drawer, I'd pulled out a beautiful Christmas ornament. It was a wooden rocking horse. There were tons of ornaments in that drawer, but something about that particular piece had brought back special memories. I couldn't put my finger on it, but I'd thought that that ornament was beautiful. I'd looked through the rest of the drawer, but my eyes had kept going back to that horse.

It was getting very late, so I'd picked up the rocking horse and left Grandma's room. I'd promised myself that I'd return the next day and begin the arduous task of packing up her belongings. I'd set the piece on the living room table, admiring the fine detail of the ornament.

Grandma had been diagnosed four years earlier with cancer, and the doctor had told her that she wasn't going to live longer than five years. Even after she'd gotten that depressing news, she was cheerful.

"We're all going to die at one time or another," she'd reminded me. "We just don't know when. I consider myself kind of blessed, because I know that I'm going to see my Savior soon. So try to smile and enjoy the rest of the time that you have with me."

My grandmother had lived life to the fullest during her last years. She'd traveled as much as her fragile body had allowed. And she wouldn't let me talk about her cancer, because she knew that discussing it had always brought tears to my eyes.

As I'd walked into the kitchen to talk to Cliff, he'd turned to me. "Honey, you have to snap out of this. I know how close you were to your grandmother, and I know how much you loved her. She wouldn't want you moping around the house like this, though. You're just barely surviving, sweetheart. You're not living your life to the fullest. She wouldn't want that," he said.

"I know, but I can't seem to get over her death," I told him. "She was sick for a long time. I knew it was coming, but her death hurt me so deeply. She was the only family that I had left. She raised me after my mother abandoned me to pursue her life of drugs. Cliff, I don't know if I can do this without her." I'd started to cry.

"You still have me," he murmured. "Your grandmother is with you, honey, and she will always be with you, in your heart," he said. "Please, baby—you can't go on like this. You're going to make yourself sick."

"I miss her so much," I whispered.

94

Cliff took me in his arms. "I know you do, honey, but you will get through this. Why don't you investigate some support groups, or get counseling at the church?" he suggested.

I'd looked at Cliff as though he were crazy. "I don't need a support group—or any counseling. I will get through this by myself!" I snapped, a little more harshly than I should have. As soon as I'd seen the look on Cliff's face, I'd realized that my words had hurt him deeply. "Cliff, I'm sorry. I shouldn't have spoken to you that way. It's just that I can't seem to get it together."

Cliff didn't respond to my statement, but he'd tried to lighten the mood by telling me about a party that his coworker was throwing. "My friend from work, Grant, is having a party at his house. He invited us, and I think it would be a good idea for us to go."

"Cliff, I'm really not in the party mood. I'll rather stay home by myself and do some work around the house," I told him.

"You may change your mind before the party. It's not for a couple of weeks yet. When do you want to help Tommy and me take down the Christmas tree? It's the end of January, and the tree is still up."

Tommy, our six-year-old son, was the light of my life. He'd been born shortly after my grandmother had come to live with us. Christmas was his favorite time of the year, and I'd hated to spoil it for him, but I wasn't in the mood to do anything. "I think you and Tommy are going to have to do that without me. I'm not up to it this year," I said.

Cliff shot me a strange look. "Tommy is going to be very disappointed. That's one of the few things that we do as a family. It signifies the end of another year," he reminded me.

"I know he'll be disappointed, but I'll talk to him and make him understand." I'd hoped that Cliff would change the subject.

"I'm going to bed now. I have an early meeting. I need to be at my best." He gave me a kiss on my cheek, and then he walked toward the bedroom. "Are you going to stay up, or are you coming to bed?"

"I'm right behind you," I told him.

As soon as my head had hit the pillow, I'd quickly fallen into a deep sleep. . . .

"Grandma!" I called, running up to my grandmother. "Look what I found over there," I said, handing her a beautiful flower that I'd found in the garden. "It's for you, Grandma, because I love you so much."

"I love you, too, my little sunshine," Grandma said, picking me up and sitting me on her lap. "Honey, there's something that I need to tell you. Grandma needs for you to be a big girl about this."

"Sure, Grandma, what is it?" I asked.

With a serious expression on her face, Grandma had begun to

speak. "Sunshine, you know how much you mean to me, and how much I love being with you, right?"

"Right, Grandma," I said. "You're so much fun to be with."

"You are, too." She'd pinched my cheek. "But Grandma has to go away for a very long time."

"Grandma, where are you going? Will I ever see you again?" I asked.

"Honey, I'm going to a big, peaceful place where I won't have to worry about any pain or sadness anymore. And honey, I'm afraid that you won't see me again. Not until it's your time."

I'd started crying and Grandma had taken me in her arms.

"Don't cry, my little sunshine. Grandma will always be with you, in your heart." Then, she'd sat me on the seat next to her, and she'd stood up and started walking away.

"Grandma, you're leaving now?" I was shocked.

"I have to go, honey. Take care of yourself. I love you, and please—stop crying."

She didn't look back, but I'd kept calling her name: "Grandma! Grandma, please come back!"

That's the way I'd awoken—screaming in my husband's arms. He'd hugged me to him tightly.

"Honey, you were having a bad dream," he told me.

"It was about Grandma. She was telling me that she had to go away, and that she was leaving me. I was calling her to come back, but she ignored me."

"Honey, you have to get some professional help with this. You can't go on this way," Cliff insisted.

"I know, Cliff. But please, give me a little more time."

"Honey, take all the time you need. I'm just afraid that you're going to have a breakdown."

"I'll be fine. Listen, I'm going in the kitchen to put on some coffee for us while you get ready for work," I said.

I'd walked into the kitchen and Tommy was there already, sitting in his chair.

"Good morning, Mommy," Tommy mumbled, rubbing the sleep out of his eyes.

"Good morning, Tommy. How did you sleep last night?" I asked.

"I slept okay. Mommy, what are we having for breakfast?"

"Sweetheart, I don't feel like cooking this morning. Can you pour yourself some cereal?"

"Okay, Mommy, but I'll need help pouring the milk. You know that I always end up spilling the milk all over the place," Tommy warned me.

I'd laughed at his simple statement. "I'll help you in a minute."

I'd watched Tommy reach for the cereal on the counter. Grandma already had been living there when Tommy was born, and she had been so thrilled at the new addition to our family. The day that I'd gone into labor, Grandma had insisted on going to the hospital with me. Throughout the entire process, she was at my side.

Walking to the bathroom, I'd bumped into my husband, who was running around the house getting ready for work. "How come you're not dressed, Susan?"

"I really don't feel like doing anything today," I admitted.

"Sweetheart, you have a family to think about," Cliff reminded me gently, giving me a hug.

"I'm not neglecting my family. You're here for Tommy, too," I said irritably.

"Of course I am, but he needs his mommy."

"I know," I admitted. "Lately, I haven't spent as much time with Tommy as I used to, but I will from now on—I promise. I just have to get things straight in my mind."

"Tommy isn't the only one that you haven't been spending time with lately," Cliff teased, with that "I'm-in-the-mood-for-love" expression sparkling in his eyes.

I loved my husband so much, but I just wasn't in the mood for sex just then. I'd brushed him off, promising him a night to remember.

"I'm running late for work, anyway. But I'll hold you to your word later. Tonight," Cliff said, picking up his briefcase.

"Tonight—I promise."

Later, I'd waved good-bye to Cliff and Tommy as they were walking out the door. I knew that I had to go grocery shopping, but I'd had little energy left. I figured that if I lay down for a while, I would summon up enough energy to do my daily chores. As I was lying on my bed, I'd tossed and turned. I couldn't think of anything else except Grandma, and how she used to sing me little lullabies to help me fall asleep. Tears had come to my eyes and started rolling down my face.

I must have been more tired than I'd thought, because when the ringing telephone had awakened me, I'd looked at the clock. It was already noon. I'd answered the phone in a groggy voice. It was Cliff, asking me if I would like to meet him for lunch in about an hour.

I'd looked at myself, and was about to turn him down. Suddenly, though, I'd changed my mind. "Would it be okay if we meet in an hour and a half? I'm in the middle of some cleaning, and I have to take a shower and get dressed before I leave." Lately, I hadn't been spending quality time with him, and I'd felt that I should at least meet him for lunch. I didn't want him to know that I'd been sleeping all day.

"That's fine, honey."

After I'd hung up the phone with him, I'd jumped in the shower to get ready for my lunch date. I'd put on the first thing that I'd pulled out of the closet and applied some makeup.

Walking down the street on my way to his office, I'd heard someone call my name. I turned around and stared into the eyes of a childhood friend—Nancy. We had been like sisters at one time, but, one day, Nancy's attitude had became cold toward me. I'd never known why, and she would never say anything. Nancy had been raised by her grandmother, too, after her mother had died. But, unlike me, her grandmother hadn't been very nice to her. She'd always spoken in a nasty tone to Nancy in front of our friends, and that had embarrassed her. Her grandmother wouldn't buy her anything that she'd wanted. And she would constantly remind Nancy of how expensive it was to get her the things that she needed.

When we were growing up, I'd always noticed a look of envy in her eyes when she'd observed my grandmother and me together. I'd always made an attempt to be closer to her, but after a while, she didn't want to be my friend anymore. By the time we'd reached our late teens, she'd moved out of the neighborhood, and I'd lost contact with her for years. Within the last two years, we'd revived our friendship. Although she traveled most of the year with her job, we'd managed to keep in touch.

"What are you doing in this neck of the woods?" she asked.

"I'm going to meet my husband for lunch," I explained.

"So, how have you been? I haven't seen you since your grandmother's funeral. I miss you. I know we've talked on the phone a couple of times, but that's not the same."

"I know. I miss you, too. But I've been dealing with a lot since her death," I admitted.

"She was such a sweet person. I know how close you were. I remember how I felt when my grandmother died, when I was nineteen. I thought my world was going to come to an end. I cried every night for practically six months. I neglected everything—even my boyfriend. He talked me into going to counseling to learn how to deal with my grief. Then, I started going to church, and it was there that I learned how to pray. My boyfriend and I still broke up, but it had nothing to do with that. My grandmother will always be in my heart, but I learned how to get over the pain and grief. It's not good for you, or for the people around you."

"That's the truth," I agreed. "I know that, but I can't seem to shake these feelings of grief."

"Have you spoken to a professional about your feelings?" she asked.

"No, I haven't," I admitted. "I don't think that I'm ready for that right now."

"Well, girl, take care of yourself, and your family. I have to finish this last-minute shopping for my boss's New Year's Eve party."

"It was good to see you," I said, walking toward Cliff's office.

Maybe she's right, I thought. I'd decided that in time, I would speak to someone. First, though, I wanted to work through some things for myself. Although Nancy had seemed to be concerned about my grief, her sympathy hadn't quite reached her eyes. If she hadn't been a friend of mine, I would have said that there was a coldness there. I didn't linger on that thought for too long, though. I was pretty sure that it'd been just my imagination.

As I was walking into my husband's office building, I'd seen something that had sent chills racing up and down my spine. It was an elderly woman who was about my grandmother's height. She'd worn her hair in a style that was similar to my grandmother's, and she was wearing a familiar coat and the same kind of shoes. When I saw her, I wasn't able to move. It wasn't until I'd gotten close to her that I'd realized that her facial features didn't resemble my grandmother's at all. She'd smiled at me as I'd passed her

My legs were shaking, and it wasn't until I'd gotten on the elevator that I'd noticed that I was crying. Suddenly, I was no longer in the mood to have lunch with Cliff. I'd called him on my cell phone and told him that I'd started feeling nauseous on my way to meet him, and that I was going home.

I'd heard a little skepticism in his voice as he'd told me to take it easy and rest for the remainder of the afternoon.

I'd felt badly about lying to my husband, but I wasn't in the mood for conversation. I'd just wanted to go home and get into bed.

As soon as I'd gotten in the door, I'd heard the phone ring. I hadn't planned on answering it, but when I'd heard Cliff's voice on the answering machine, I'd changed my mind

"Hello," I said.

"Hi, honey. It's me, Cliff. I just called to tell you that I'm picking up Tommy on my way home from work."

"Thanks, sweetheart. I forgot to make arrangements for that," I admitted.

"It's no problem. You just get some rest."

"I will," I promised. "I love you."

Hanging up the telephone, I'd walked into my bedroom and started pulling off my clothes. Before I was able to get into bed, though, the telephone rang again. I'd answered the phone, but there was only heavy breathing on the other end. I'd kept saying "hello," but still, no one answered. Remembering the telephone call that I'd received earlier, I'd hung up the phone.

I was too anxious to sleep, so I'd gotten out of bed and started reading a book. Cliff and Tommy came in a few hours later.

A few minutes later, Cliff walked into the room and asked if I was feeling any better.

"I am. Maybe I caught a twenty-four-hour virus or something."

"Maybe," he said dubiously. "Sweetheart, there's something that I want to talk to you about. I wanted to talk to you earlier, but I didn't want to bring it up when you weren't feeling well."

"Sure, go ahead," I said.

"Earlier today, right before you called me, my coworker told me that you were on your way upstairs. He explained that he'd seen you in the lobby. Apparently, you were closer to my office than you told me. How come you didn't want to meet me for lunch?"

I'd really felt badly then, and I'd decided to tell him the truth. I'd told him how shaken up I'd been after the incident with the elderly woman who'd resembled my grandmother.

He'd tried to remain calm, but I could see how frustrated he was getting with the situation.

"Honey, I think we need to go and see someone tomorrow. I'm calling your physician to get a recommendation for a good grief counselor. This has been going on for far too long, and it's getting out of hand."

I hadn't liked his last statement, but I had agreed with him—I had been feeling that way for far too long. "You're right, honey," I told him. "I will see a counselor."

I'd realized that his concern for my mental health had intensified after I'd told him about the phone call that I'd received earlier.

The next day, I'd proceeded to get Tommy ready for school. After Cliff had eaten a hearty breakfast, he'd kissed me good-bye, and then, he and Tommy had left for work and school.

I didn't have any plans for the day, so I'd decided to take a long, leisurely bubble bath. After I'd started running the water and had poured in the bubbles, the telephone rang. Thinking that it was Cliff, I'd rushed to the telephone.

"Hello," I said.

The caller on the other end didn't say anything immediately. Then, finally, the person had spoken. "Good morning, sunshine. How are you this morning?" It was the same voice of the person who'd called a few days earlier.

My palms had started sweating. "Who is this and why are you doing this to me?" I screamed into the phone.

"Doing what, sunshine? I'm just calling you to say good morning. What's the matter?"

Tears had started forming in my eyes, so I'd just hung up the telephone.

Too upset to do anything, I'd sat on the couch, crying. The phone had rung again, but that time, I'd decided not to answer it, thinking that it might have been the caller again. I'd let the answering machine pick it up, and it was Cliff. I'd picked up the phone and, immediately, he'd known that there was something wrong.

"Honey, that person called again," I told him.

"What did you say?" he asked.

"I asked why they were doing this to me, but they didn't say anything. Honey, what's going on? Can't we put a tracer on the line or something?"

"Sweetie, calm down. I think it's a prank caller, and that you shouldn't give too much thought to it. If it makes you feel any better, I'll buy a caller ID and maybe you can get the number."

"It's probably blocked. I'll feel better if we could get the number, though."

I could hear the skepticism in his voice when he'd continued. "Let's hear what the grief counselor has to say."

I didn't press the issue any further. I'd just agreed with him and hung up the phone. Before I could move from the spot, though, the phone had rung again. I'd let the answering machine pick up again, and it was Cliff. I wondered why he was calling again.

"Honey, it's me," he said, after I'd picked up. "I called back to tell you that I love you. I also wanted to know if you wanted me to pick up Tommy today."

"No, I need to get out of the house for a while, so I'll do it. We'll probably go out for ice cream, so don't expect us to be home when you get here."

"Okay, honey. I'll see you later.

"Take care, sweetie. I love you, too."

Later, I'd gone to pick up Tommy from school, and he was the first student on line.

"Mommy!" he cried, running up to me with his arms outstretched. "What are you doing here today? I thought that Daddy was going to pick me up."

"I wanted to pick you up so we could go out for pizza or ice cream—whatever you want. Is that okay with you, sir?"

"Yummy!" Tommy exclaimed, rubbing his tummy. He knew when he did that, I always smiled, so he'd made a point to do it when he knew that I was feeling a little sad. I'd laughed at him and grabbed his hand.

"So, what do you want, pizza or ice cream—or both?"

"Both, Mommy. You know that those are my favorites."

I didn't know if it was a good idea to give him both, but then again, I wouldn't have to worry about giving him dinner once I got home. "Let's go for it!" I told him.

We walked down to the pizza place on the corner, which also had video games. I knew that we were going to be in there for a while.

While Tommy was chatting away about his day, we'd run into Nancy.

"Why, hello!" she said.

"Hi, Nancy. It's weird running into you again. Sometimes I don't see you for months at a time, and now, I'm seeing you twice in a week. What a surprise!" I exclaimed.

"I hope it's a welcome surprise," she commented.

"Of course. It's always good to see you."

She'd looked down and noticed Tommy at my side. I could see that Tommy was a little hesitant about talking to her, but he was polite.

"Where are you two going?" she asked.

"Well, I just picked him up from school and now, we're going to get pizza and ice cream. We're going to spend a little time together."

"That sounds good. Do you two mind if I join in on the fun? I haven't eaten anything at all today, and I don't think I can take another step without any food."

"Sure, you can join us," I told her. I really didn't want her to eat with us, but I'd thought that it would be rude of me not to include her.

We'd walked into the pizza place and put in an order for a large pie. Nancy asked me how I was doing, in reference to what we'd spoken about the other day.

"I'm a little better. Cliff—" I'd looked at Tommy and he'd seemed very bored, so I'd given him some money to play the video games. He'd skipped away happily.

"I didn't want him to hear this," I told Nancy.

"I'm sorry," she said.

"That's fine. But as I was saying, Cliff made an appointment for me to get some counseling tomorrow."

"That's good. Maybe that will help you to deal with the pain," she told me.

"Maybe." I didn't want to go into details about the calls I had been receiving. "Other than that, I'm okay. What about you?"

"Well, I've been very busy at work. As a matter of fact, I'm going out of town in a couple of weeks. I'm so tired of traveling. I'm thinking about taking a leave of absence."

"Where are you going?" I asked.

"I'm going to Paris for three weeks. There's a client over there who needs our assistance."

"That sounds exciting."

"It sounds nice, but like I said, I'm just tired of traveling. I want to settle down with a husband and have children, like you. I'm tired of coming home to an empty house every night."

"Being a stay-at-home mom and wife is great. I love it, but it gets boring at times," I admitted. "Since Grandma's death, I've been thinking about getting a part-time job to keep myself busy."

Nancy shook her head. "Girl, why would you want to do that? If I had a wonderful family like yours, I would want to stay home all the time."

I'd laughed. "It is nice to be home when they get home from school and work. Hey, are you seeing anyone right now?"

"No, I can't find a decent man to save my soul. I remember that you never had a problem getting a boyfriend when we were growing up. My childhood wasn't as stable as yours, so I always had trouble getting a boyfriend." She'd started laughing to herself.

"What's so funny?" I asked.

"Do you remember that time when we were talking, and your grandmother came outside, and called you 'sunshine' in front of your boyfriend? I've never seen anyone turn as red before as you did then. She was so funny. I remember her always asking you about your day." Suddenly, Nancy looked down at her watch. "Oh, I have to get out of here. I have an appointment with a client in thirty minutes, and it's across town." She gave me some money to pay for her portion of the pizza.

"Take care, Nancy," I said. "I hope you make it on time."

"Thanks for letting me join you. Please tell Tommy that I said good-bye."

I'd always enjoyed talking to Nancy, but every time I'd finished spending time with her, I'd always gotten a funny feeling that she was fishing for something. It was almost as if we were still kids. At that moment, Tommy had come running back over to the table, and he'd picked up a slice of pizza.

"Mom, did your friend leave?"

"Yes, she did, sweetie. Don't eat too much pizza, or you won't have room for ice cream."

"Mom, I didn't like her. She spoke to me and everything, but I just didn't like her," he told me.

It was a little odd that he'd said that, because I'd felt almost the same way. "What is it that you didn't like, Tommy?" I asked.

"I don't know—it was just something. Anyway, can we take some ice cream home to Daddy?" Tommy asked, changing the subject.

"Yes, we can. How about if we wrap up the slices that are left? Then, we'll go to the ice cream place and order a half gallon of mint chocolate chip ice cream."

"Sounds good to me. That's Daddy's favorite—and mine, too!" he exclaimed.

"Come on, let's go home," I said.

On our way home, we were both lost in our own thoughts. My

mind was still stuck on the fact that he'd said that he didn't like Nancy. I'd wanted to ask him more about that, but I'd thought that it would be better to let it go.

The next day, I'd gone to my first counseling session alone. Cliff had offered again to go with me, but I'd told him that I'd wanted to do it alone. He did drive me to the office, though.

The counselor was nothing like I'd expected. She was a young woman, and her certificates and awards were hanging on the walls of her office.

We'd both settled on her leather couch with our cups of tea, and I'd told her all about my grandma. I'd even told her about the phone calls that I'd been receiving. "Now, I'm depressed a lot, and I'm starting to neglect my family," I finished.

"Do you have any enemies who would enjoy hurting you like this?" she asked.

"None that I can think of. As far as I know, I get along well with everybody, and everybody I know seems to like me."

"Most of the time, our enemies are the people who we believe are our friends. I'm not too concerned about how you're dealing with your grandmother's death, because your reaction is normal. I am concerned about these telephone calls. There's one thing that you need to do, though, in order to come to terms with her death."

I'd looked curiously at the counselor. "What's that?"

"You need to clean up her room. Donate her clothes to a shelter. Your grandmother's memory will always be in your heart. By clearing her room, you won't be erasing the memories. She will live forever here—and here," she said, pointing to her head and to her heart.

"Maybe you're right," I murmured.

"I recommend that you do it as soon as possible; then we can deal with other things. You'll be able to move on with your life and become the vibrant person that you once were. You can either do it by yourself, or with your husband, but it needs to be done soon."

"I will," I promised. "It just seems so strange, to be going through her things."

"I understand completely, but you need to move on with your life and take care of your family."

After I'd left her office, I had felt a little better. I'd called Cliff from my cell phone, just like he'd asked me to do, and I'd told him what had happened.

"When are you going to clean her room?" Cliff asked.

"I don't know, but I'll do it by myself."

"Okay, honey. Listen, I just wanted to know how the visit went. I'll talk to you later, because I have a meeting to prepare for. I love you."

"I love you, too," I told him.

104

I had taken the long way home, thinking about what I had to do. When I got home, I went into Grandma's room for the second time and looked around. I started picking up her little trinkets and putting them down. Then, I'd opened her closet and admired all of her beautiful clothes. One by one, I'd taken everything off the hangers and laid them neatly on the bed. After I'd gathered all of her clothes together, I'd gotten an old suitcase. I'd neatly folded up her things and placed them inside the suitcase. When I'd gotten to her favorite sweater, the tears had started falling down the sides of my face freely. I couldn't hold back any longer. I must have sat there for about twenty minutes, before I'd gathered up enough strength to go on.

An hour later, I'd closed the suitcase and carried it to the front door, vowing to call her church tomorrow to donate the clothes.

Then I'd looked on the top of her bureau at the little trinkets and perfumes, wondering if I could get any more done that night. This is something I needed to do, to get myself together and to go on with my life, I told myself as I picked up a small bag and carefully placed all the bottles of perfume inside. I did take a few of the bottles of perfume and the rocking horse made of wood for myself. I'd decided to donate the other stuff, since I didn't have any living relatives to share Grandma's things with.

By the time I'd finished, Cliff had came home with Tommy in tow. Apparently, Tommy was sleepy or asleep already, because he wasn't behind Cliff when he entered the room.

"Honey, you cleaned this room already?" he asked.

"Yes, it was something that had to be done," I said.

"Yes, it had to be done," he agreed, holding his arms out to me. "How do you feel?"

"Well, of course, I'm a little depressed, but I know that Grandma will always be with me."

"Yes, she will. She will always be a part of your heart. These are just her material things that you're getting rid of—not her memory. You know, I love your courage for doing this."

"Thank-you, honey," I murmured.

"No, thank you for being who you are. Come on, we can finish up tomorrow. I have something to show you."

"Really? I like surprises. I could use one right about now."

I'd walked into the dining room, and Tommy was standing there with his little finger pointed to a beautifully set table, adorned with several cartons of Chinese food.

"Tommy, sweetie, this is wonderful! Did you do this all by yourself, or did Daddy help?"

"Daddy paid for the food, but I set the table all by myself," he told me proudly.

"You did a great job," I said, giving him a kiss on the cheek. I'd looked at my husband and smiled. "Thank you," I mouthed to him. He gave me a kiss and pulled out a chair for me.

We'd talked about each other's day, and by the time we'd finished eating, I'd noticed how sleepy Tommy was getting. "It's almost someone's bedtime," I said.

"I know, Mommy. I'm getting very sleepy."

"Come on, sweetie. Let's give you a bath and put you to bed."

"No, I'll do it," my husband insisted. "You had a busy day."

"Thanks, Cliff. I'll meet you in the bedroom," I whispered, using my most seductive voice.

"I'll be there in about twenty minutes," Cliff said. He gave me a swat on my behind. I'd laughed at his enthusiasm.

While they were gone, I'd started cleaning the table. As I was taking the last carton off the table, I was interrupted by the ringing of the telephone.

I'd answered, but no one said anything. As I was about to hang up, I'd heard the voice on the other end. "Sunshine, I'm here."

I'd closed my eyes, hoping that it wasn't real.

"Sunshine, are you still there?" the voice screamed out.

Frightened, I'd hung up the phone. I was a nervous wreck. I couldn't do anything. So I'd just turned off the lights and gone into the bedroom.

Soon after I'd gotten into bed, Cliff had come in with a big smile on his face. Once he'd seen my cold expression, the smile had disappeared. "What's the matter, babe?" he asked.

"I just got another call," I explained.

Cliff had sat on the edge of the bed. "Was it the same caller, or someone else?"

"No, it was the same person. Cliff, why is someone doing this to me? Who hates me so much?"

"Shush," Cliff crooned, holding me in his arms. "I don't know, honey, but we will get to the bottom of this."

Cliff just lay there, holding me in his arms. He knew that I wasn't in the mood to make love to him that night, and I'd loved him for not pushing me.

The next morning, I'd woken up in his arms. It was Saturday, and I'd promised Tommy that he could go to the movies with his best friend and his mother. Later, he was going to stay the night. I'd looked at the clock by my nightstand and seen that I had another few hours before he had to be ready. I'd looked over at my husband, who was sleeping so peacefully. At least, I'd thought that he was sleeping until he'd grabbed me by the waist and kissed me on the lips.

"Honey, I thought you were asleep," I said.

"I know you did. Hey, we have a few hours before Tommy has to leave, so let's have some time to ourselves now."

"What do you have in mind?" I teased. "From the smile on your face, I guess that's a silly question."

"Yes, you're right." He grinned.

Cliff began stroking me as he gave me a passion-filled kiss. I'd returned his kiss with just as much passion. He'd just started to pull my short nightie over my head when we'd heard the familiar knock at our bedroom door.

"Yes, Tommy?" I asked.

"Mommy, did you forget that I'm supposed to go to the movies with Brendan and his mother today? Then, I'm staying over at their house."

"No, Tommy, I didn't forget. You have a few hours before you go. Why don't you go and watch a little television?" I suggested.

"Mommy, I think that I should start getting ready now."

"Tommy, go and watch television and I'll help you to get ready in about a half an hour."

I'd heard the sigh in his voice, but he'd walked away.

"Now, where were we, big boy?" I asked, turning toward Cliff.

He'd had no problems reminding me.

Later that morning, I'd helped Tommy to get ready for his afternoon. By the time Brendan's mother had arrived, Tommy was ready to go. I'd chatted with Brendan and his mom for a while, and then they'd left. Tommy was so excited that he'd barely kissed his father and me good-bye.

"Well, we have the day to ourselves, honey. What do you want to do?" Cliff asked.

"Well, I was thinking that since it's such a nice day, we could have a little picnic."

"That sounds good. How long will it take you to get ready?"

"About an hour. We can pick up some salads, sandwiches, and drinks at the deli on the corner."

An hour later, we were on our way to the deli. We held hands.

We had a romantic afternoon together, with a lot of talking and romance. That afternoon, I'd forgotten about everything and everyone except my husband. We were the only two people in the world.

That night, we'd made love the way we used to, with a lot of passion and sensitivity. Afterward, I'd slept like a baby.

The next day was Sunday and Tommy came home, all excited about his outing. He'd followed me to the kitchen and was telling me all about it when the telephone rang. My hands were too wet to get the phone, so Tommy had picked it up for me.

"Hello," he answered. "Sunshine? Who's that?" I heard him say.

107

I can't believe this, I thought. The same caller got my son on the phone.

After he'd hung up, he'd looked at me strangely. "Mom, who were they talking about?"

"Don't worry about it, baby. It was probably the wrong number."

"Maybe, but it sounded like the lady we saw the other day. She was just making her voice sound like one of the people on my cartoons."

"What lady are you talking about?" I asked.

"You know, the lady that I told you I didn't like," he reminded me.

"Honey, how would you know? You didn't hear her talk that much."

"I heard enough. I watch a lot of cartoons, Mommy." Not realizing how important that conversation was to me, Tommy went on. "Mom, what are we having for dinner tonight?"

"Chicken, carrots, and mashed potatoes. Honey, go in your bedroom and play until dinner is ready. Please call your father for me, too."

"Okay, Mom."

While he was gone, I'd sat down and thought about what my son had just said. Why in the world would Nancy do something like that to me? I'd thought about it for a long time, and I couldn't think of any reason why she'd want to hurt me. He has to be mistaken about the voice, I told myself.

A few minutes later, Cliff walked into the kitchen and asked me what was wrong. I'd told him about the call, and about what Tommy had said.

"Honey, I only met Nancy once, but she didn't seem as if she could do something so evil."

"This doesn't make any sense to me, either. But, right now, I'm willing to check out any lead that I have. That caller is driving me crazy."

"How are we supposed to check this out?" he asked.

"I don't know. Maybe I can 'accidentally' run into her again, and somehow ask her questions that only the caller would know the answers to."

Then, as I was about to get up from the table, a thought had come to me. I'd almost fallen back into my chair.

"Sweetheart, what's the matter?" Cliff asked.

"The other day when I saw her, she started telling me about a time when my grandmother had called me 'sunshine' in front of my boyfriend at the time. I remember that day clearly. Grandma made it a point never to call me that in front of my friends. How would she know Grandma's pet name for me?"

108

"I have no idea, but I don't think that you should try to run into her. I think we should pay her a visit tomorrow. There's no time for more games. Do you know where she works?"

"Yes, I do. She works in a building in the business district."

"Good. We can go there together tomorrow morning."

For the rest of the day, I was jittery and nervous. That night, I didn't get a good night's rest.

The next morning after we'd dropped Tommy off at school, Cliff and I had gone to Nancy's office. I'd found the floor that she worked on, but her receptionist had informed us that she was running a little late. She'd asked us if we wanted to wait for her. We told her that we would, and took a seat in the waiting area.

When Nancy had seen us sitting there, I'd thought that she was going to have a heart attack right on the spot. After she'd gotten over her initial shock, she'd asked us to come into her office.

We'd followed behind her, and she'd closed the door after we were seated. "Susan, it's so nice to see you. I'm glad that you're here. I'm surprised to see that you brought your husband," she said, acknowledging him for the first time. "Is everything okay?"

"Let's stop playing games, Nancy. You know why I'm here, and I want you to stop it now."

"Stop what, Susan? What are you talking about?"

"You know very well that I'm talking about the phone calls," I snapped.

"What phone calls?" Nancy asked, confused.

"Sunshine, how are you this morning?" I imitated her. "Stop it, Nancy. Why are you doing this?"

Suddenly, her face hardened and her voice became thick with emotion. "You know why I'm doing it!" she said angrily. "When we were growing up, you had everything that you ever wanted, while I had nothing. My grandmother was cruel to me, but you and your precious grandmother didn't even care. We were good friends once. Then you turned your back on me."

I couldn't believe that Nancy had been holding a grudge against me for so many years. "Nancy, I was just as young as you were at that time. What did you want me to do? What did you want Grandma to do? You were in your grandmother's custody, and you never told anyone about being mistreated."

"Whatever, Susan. It doesn't matter now," she muttered.

"Nancy, I hope that you get some help for this. If I get another phone call from you, I'm calling the police. You don't realize how this is tearing me up. How dare you try to hurt me this way!"

"You don't have to worry about me calling you again. You're not worth my time!" she screamed.

My husband had led me out of the office, and I'd kept my composure together until I'd reached the car. Then I'd broken into tears. Cliff had comforted me, and we'd headed home in silence.

Later that afternoon, Cliff had offered to go and pick up Tommy from school. I was happy about that because I'd needed some time by myself. After he'd closed the door, I'd just sat on the couch, staring at the almost-empty Christmas tree that Cliff and Tommy had just about finished clearing. As I was looking at the tree, something looked different about it.

The tree was lighting up the house like none of our trees ever had before. There was a glowing light around it—almost like a halo around an angel's head. I'd walked over to the tree. I'd noticed a decoration there that I knew I hadn't put there—and neither had Cliff or Tommy. It was the wooden rocking horse that had belonged to my grandma. I'd picked it up and held it close to my heart. At that moment, I'd known, without a doubt, that Grandma was watching over me. She was telling me that I shouldn't start off the year by still holding on to things that I could not change. I'd cried like a baby—but that time, they were tears of joy. I began taking down the rest of the decorations, still holding on to the rocking horse.

A year has passed and, true to her word, Nancy never called again. I'd never heard from her, or seen her, again. I'd continued my counseling sessions for a few more months, and then both the counselor and I had agreed that I was able to function normally, so I'd stopped going.

Cliff, Tommy, and I are doing more family things together. And, as for Grandma—I may have removed all of her material possessions from the house, but her memory will live in my heart forever.

THE END

I RAISED A KILLER

I was jolted out of a deep sleep by the frenzied barking of Chipper, our family dog. Dragging myself out from under the covers, I'd groped in the dark for my robe. A glance at the digital alarm clock had shown me that it was only five-thirty in the morning. What on earth was that darn dog going on about? He never barked without a good reason.

"There must be someone in the yard. Chipper is going crazy," I mumbled.

I'd poked my husband, Glenn, in the ribs and tried to awaken him. He'd simply grunted and rolled over onto his other side. A flash of anger had surged through me. I was tired of always having to be the one who took care of things around the house. I knew that Glenn wasn't well, but I'd hoped that he would at least try to do something to help out on occasion.

"Chipper, be quiet," I mumbled as I felt my way down the staircase in the darkness.

As I'd reached the back door and unlocked it, I'd heard the dog yelp. It had sounded as if someone had kicked him. A bubble of fear had burst inside of me, and I'd grabbed for the baseball bat that my son, Josh, had left laying on the floor. My trusty weapon over my shoulder, I'd started to open the door.

Suddenly, the bat was wrenched from my hand, and the door was thrust open. I'd stumbled back from the force of it. Before I was able to do or to say anything, a group of men had burst in and filled the hallway. The bat was ripped from my hands and I'd found myself thrust up against the wall, my face pushed against the woodwork by a rough hand at the base of my neck.

Oh, God, I thought, it's a home invasion. My legs had started to tremble and my stomach was churning with nausea.

"Are you the only one in the house?" a man asked.

Hands had spun me around and I'd stared into hard, emotionless eyes. I couldn't take it in. The room was full of men in uniforms, with bulletproof vests covering their chests. Some of them held weapons— handguns, drawn and ready.

"Are you alone?" he went on.

I'd dragged my gaze back to the man in front of me. It had required all of my concentration to shake my head at his question. Speaking at that moment was a physical impossibility. My mouth was dry, and I couldn't swallow.

After a nod from the man who'd held me captive, men had begun to stream up the staircase and invade the safe haven of my home. I'd opened my mouth and begun to call out to Glenn, but the look on the man's face had warned me to keep quiet.

"What's going on? Why are you here?" I managed to whisper, my heart pounding furiously in my chest.

"Do you own that car that's parked out front?" he asked.

"Yes, it's my husband's car." I'd frowned. What did our vehicle have to do with the police bursting into our house at that time of the morning? "We haven't done anything wrong. Why are you doing this?" I asked again.

"Your vehicle was used in the commission of a crime last night," he informed me.

"No, that's impossible. We didn't use it last. . . ."

My words had trailed off as I'd remembered that Josh had used the car the previous night. We had all been sitting in the family room the night before when the phone had rung. Josh had answered it. It was Ace, a friend of the family—or Arnold, to those who didn't know his nickname. We had known him for years. Although he was quite a few years older than Josh, the two were firm friends, and had spent a lot of time together. I'd had to admit that I'd often wondered why a man in his early forties had wanted to spend so much time with a twenty-one-year-old young man.

Ace had lost his license for drunk driving, and he'd often asked Josh to drive him places. The night before, he'd needed to go pick up some money from an acquaintance who'd supposedly owed him a large amount of cash. I'd thought nothing of it when Josh had told me that he was driving Ace over to the guy's apartment. Josh had even asked if he could borrow his father's car, as his was low on gas.

I had never been able to sleep well until I was certain that the children were home, despite the fact that they were all young adults. Bryce, Josh's older brother, had been sound asleep when I'd heard our vehicle in the driveway. It must have been about one in the morning, and I'd assumed that Ace and Josh had gone back to his place for a few drinks before Josh had come home. He'd seemed to take a long time to come inside. But, once I'd known that Josh was in bed, I'd settled back down and drifted off to sleep. Until I'd heard Chipper barking, at least.

"If you didn't use it, who did?" the officer barked.

"Please, can we go upstairs?" I pleaded. "I'm worried about my husband. He has a heart condition."

For some reason, it was bothering me that I didn't know the man's name. Who the heck cares, at this point in the proceedings? I thought. My son was in trouble, and I had to help him.

He'd indicated the staircase. I'd stumbled away from the wall and made my way upstairs, conscious all the while of the heavy hand on my shoulder. Glenn was standing in the middle of the room, surrounded by officers. I'd edged over to his side, outraged suddenly that they hadn't even allowed him to drag some trousers over his boxers.

"Glenn, what's going on?" I asked as I slipped my hand in his. Then I'd thought of my sons. I'd pulled away from him. "The boys!"

The officer who'd guided me upstairs had held out his arm. "Sorry, but you'll have to stay here," he insisted. "Your sons are being questioned at the moment. You can't speak to them."

"Who the hell are you to say that I can't speak to my kids?" Glenn asked angrily.

I'd grabbed his hand again in an effort to calm him before he got too belligerent. He wasn't known for his even temper. And I knew that if he became too worked up, he could have a heart attack. He'd already had two in the past, and was waiting to undergo heart surgery.

"I'm Detective Jordan, and I'm in charge of this case," the officer said.

"What case?" Glenn demanded.

"Your vehicle was used in the commission of a crime last night. So how about telling me who was driving it?" he persisted.

"What crime? The only one who used my car was my son. He drove a friend somewhere to pick up some money," Glenn explained. "There's no crime in that."

I'd wanted to hit him. Why couldn't he have kept his mouth shut, until we'd had time to talk to Josh? He was a good father, but he had no patience with the children—or with Josh, in particular. Bryce was like his father, but, Josh, well—he was special. He was my son. Too sensitive, with the sweetest nature that anyone could have hoped for. And that was part of the problem, as far as his father was concerned.

Glenn thought that he should be a rough, tough, macho male— into football, drinking, swearing, and womanizing. Sure, Josh liked to have a drink every now and then, but he never lost control and got drunk—unlike his father and brother. And he'd always hated sports, preferring to spend his time reading and writing poetry. He'd always liked girls, too, but, at twenty-one, he wasn't into getting serious, although he had lots of female friends.

I'd peered down the hallway and seen two officers walking out of Josh's bedroom. My son was between them, his hands cuffed behind his back. One of the men came over and whispered in Detective Jordan's ear.

"Where are you taking Josh?" My voice was trembling as I'd asked the question.

Josh had looked terrified, as if he were about to cry. I'd wanted to go to him and wrap my arms about him. I'd wanted to hold him close, just as I'd done when he was younger.

"What the hell have you done now, Josh?" Glenn asked.

"I haven't done anything," Josh insisted. "I don't know what this is all about. Mom?" he asked fearfully.

I'd made a move toward him but, once again, Detective Jordan had stopped me. "Please, can't you tell us what he's supposed to have done?" I begged.

"We had a report last night about a group of five men beating up another guy on a nearby street. The witness saw them toss the victim into the back of a vehicle and took down the license-plate number. It was your vehicle, and your son was the driver. Now the victim is missing, and we believe that your son can help us."

I'd glanced over at my youngest son. "Josh?" I asked hesitantly.

"I didn't do anything, Mom. I just drove Ace up there to collect his money. I wasn't a part of anything else," he insisted.

The officers had dragged Josh into the living room and sat him down on the couch. Bryce, his brother, had sidled into the room, hugged the wall, and said nothing. His face was pale with shock. The boys might have fought all the time, like a lot of siblings did, but Bryce loved his brother. I was sure of that.

"Can I talk to him?" I whispered to the detective. As he'd nodded, I'd moved on trembling legs across the room and crouched down in front of Josh.

"Josh, tell me what happened," I said gently.

"I can't, Mom," he mumbled.

Tears had filled his eyes as he'd stared at me. I'd placed my hand on his knee. "Please, Josh, you have to tell us what happened."

"It will go a lot easier on you if you tell the truth, son," Detective Jordan added. "The person who was assaulted is a known drug user, but he's still entitled to justice. His girlfriend has reported him as missing. At the moment, you'll only be charged with assault. But if we don't find out where he is, the situation could be even more serious."

I couldn't believe it—the police were going to charge my son! "Please, Josh, tell us what happened." I could see how frightened he was. His face was pale, and his eyes were full of tears. He'd shrugged one shoulder and tried to swipe at his eyes.

"Okay," I went on, "let me start. Ace called you to take him to Medford to collect some money he was owed. You picked him up from his house. What happened next?"

"He had me stop and pick up three friends of his on the way," my son told me. "Then he directed me to a house. He told me that the guy was leaving town the next day. Then he said that he had to get his money from him before he disappeared."

"Did you go into the house?" Detective Jordan asked harshly.

Josh shook his head. "No, I stayed in the car. The rest of them went inside and, after about ten minutes or so, a guy came running out and took off down the street. Ace and his friends took off after him. They didn't hit him much. He only had a bloody nose and a few cuts over his eye. I didn't even get out of the car until they dragged him back."

"What happened then, sweetie?" I asked, my heart pounding in my chest. Even if Josh hadn't touched him, he had still been at the scene. In the eyes of the law, he would be guilty by association.

"Ace opened the back of the car, and they threw the guy in. Then they all jumped in and told me to drive."

"Why didn't you tell them to get out? That you wouldn't have anything to do with it?" I asked.

"Rex, Ace's friend, was sitting in the backseat behind me. When I said I wasn't driving anywhere, he pulled out a knife. He threatened to slit my throat if I didn't do what I was told."

"Do you remember where you drove?" Detective Jordan threw the question out, not waiting for Josh to answer. "Can you take us there?"

"I don't know the address, but I can take you to the house. When we got there, Ace told me to stay in the car. They pulled the guy from the back of the car and dragged him into a garage. Then Ace told me to take off, and to keep my mouth shut."

"And what time was that?" the detective continued.

"About midnight, I think," Josh mumbled.

"Did you come straight home?" he persisted.

Josh shook his head. "I stopped at the service station on the main highway and filled up Dad's car. Then I grabbed a sandwich and a soda. I drove back here after I'd eaten."

"And you left Ace there?" I asked.

"He was still there when I left."

While Detective Jordan had been talking to Josh, one of the other officers had obviously been on the phone to the police station. He came back into the room and beckoned to his superior. I'd tilted my head to listen to their conversation.

"Arnold Hensley's place has been checked out. His wife has no idea where he is. He didn't come home last night. And on the assumption that this guy, Rex, is Robert Conway, I had them do a check over there as well." He'd raised his eyebrows. "Guess what his wife said?"

"He didn't come home last night, either," Detective Jordan said grimly.

"That's right."

Detective Jordan turned toward Josh. "You have any idea of the names of the other two guys?" he asked.

Josh shook his head.

"Are you sure?" he asked again. "Because at the moment, you're all that we've got. You're looking at assault and kidnapping, at the very least."

Just then, another officer had entered the room, holding a broken ax handle between two fingers. "Found this in the vehicle, hidden under the backseat," he began. "Looks like there's blood on the end, and there's also blood on the carpet in the trunk of the car. It appears as though someone tried to clean it. It's all wet."

"Josh?" I'd stared at him in shock. I couldn't—wouldn't—believe that my son was a part of such a thing.

"I don't know how the ax handle got there, Mom. Honest! And I didn't clean the car. I don't know why it's wet."

I'd stood and laid my hand on Josh's head. "I believe my son," I said firmly. "He's guilty of nothing more than doing a favor for a friend."

"Sorry, Mrs. Riley, but as I said, he's all we've got. Unless he can tell us where Arnold Hensley has gone. Josh?"

When Josh shook his head again, the two officers on either side of him hauled him to his feet.

"Josh Riley, you're being charged with assault and kidnapping," the detective said. He'd nodded to the officers. "Take him out and read him his rights. Then transport him to the station."

"Glenn, do something!" I cried out to my silent husband.

He'd shrugged. "The kid got himself into trouble. Let him get himself out of it. I told you he'd come to a bad end, what with all that reading and poetry you fed him."

I'd turned and watched through the large window in the living room as the police had led my son away down the drive. They'd put him into the back of an unmarked car and slammed the door, shutting off all sight of him. Then as a large wrecker from a local salvage yard had pulled up, they'd driven away.

"We'll be taking the vehicle to forensics for analysis of the blood and further inspection," Detective Jordan informed us.

Angrily, I'd turned to face him. "You've taken my son. The car means nothing. Do what you have to do; then, get out of here."

"Do you give us permission to conduct a search of the premises for any further evidence?" he asked.

I'd nodded. What did it matter? I knew that my son wasn't guilty of anything more than being a good friend to Ace.

As I'd watched them tear apart my home, anger had started to eat at me. It burned deeply, and lodged in my heart. How dare Ace

116

have involved my boy in such a mess? He was supposed to have been a friend. He must have known what was going to happen at that house. Otherwise, why would Josh have been instructed to pick up his friends on the way?

And, suddenly, he'd gone missing, leaving my Josh to take the fall.

Finally, Detective Jordan came back into the living room. I was still standing by the window. Glenn had wandered into the kitchen, and I could hear the clatter of crockery as he'd made himself a cup of coffee. He couldn't start his day without his coffee. How could he have been thinking of something so trivial when our lives were falling apart?

"Mrs. Riley, there's a good chance that Arnold Hensley could try and contact your son," Detective Jordan began. "How do you feel about having your phones tapped, in case he does? We could get a court order, but it will be a lot quicker if you just give us your permission. If it wasn't for Hensley, your son wouldn't be involved at all."

The anger inside of me had flared up again. The detective was right, though. Without Ace, none of the horror would have been happening to my poor Josh. I'd bitten my lip and nodded. What harm could it do? And it might even help. Darn Ace for allowing this to happen! I thought furiously.

After the police had gone, I'd wandered through the house. The officers had been surprisingly neat in their search. Only Josh's room was a mess. Clothes were everywhere, the bed was stripped, and the mattress had been turned over. I'd busied myself by tidying up the mess. What else could I do? I couldn't call a lawyer for my boy until after nine o'clock.

Glenn wasn't talking to me. Or, rather, I wasn't talking to him. I was still too angry with him for not defending his son. Our marriage had been shaky for a long time. Glenn had never been there for us. He was always out with the boys for a drink, or on a fishing trip. Since he'd stopped working after the first heart attack, things had gone downhill rapidly. He'd morphed into a tyrant, using his illness to turn me into his slave. Or, maybe he'd always been like that, and I'd chosen not to acknowledge the sad truth.

On top of that, I was working full-time to bring in enough money for us to live at least reasonably comfortably. And that hadn't sat too well with Glenn, either—the fact that I was the breadwinner in the family now. He was a man who'd always belonged to the old school. He believed that a woman's place was in the home, and that the man brought in the wages.

I'd just wanted him to hold me, and to tell me that it would be

117

all right. Instead, all he was able to do was to curse Josh. Finally, I couldn't listen anymore. I wandered downstairs and sat there, staring at the telephone, willing the minutes to tick by.

As soon as nine o'clock came, I'd called the first criminal lawyer I could find in the phone book. He didn't want anything to do with my son's case, but he did give me the number of a solicitor who was willing to help me. All I'd had to do was to work out where I was going to get the money to pay him.

I'd busied myself with cleaning up the family room. I couldn't think of anything else to do. I didn't want to go outside, because I didn't want to answer any questions from the neighbors. I'd seen them all lining the street when the police had taken away Josh. More for background noise than anything else, I'd flicked on the television set and continued to tidy the room. Then I was dragged to a halt by the early morning news.

"The police have taken twenty-one-year-old Josh Riley into custody after an early-morning raid on his home. Riley is believed to be a member of a gang that attacked and beat a nineteen-year-old victim last night. The victim is still missing. He is believed to have been kidnapped by the remaining members of the gang."

My heart had started to race as the announcer's voice had rolled over me. My Josh wasn't a part of any gang! How could the announcer have said that? I'd stared at the television screen in shock as a camera had panned across the front of our house. Then there had been a shot of our car being loaded onto the transport vehicle. I'd wanted to laugh. At that point, I knew I wouldn't have to worry about the neighbors finding out. The whole street would be buzzing with gossip soon enough.

The newscaster's face had come back on the screen. I'd tried to focus—to tune out the roaring in my ears.

"Breaking news. The body of a young man has been found buried in a shallow grave in the sand dunes in Medford by a couple out for an early morning jog. It appears that some attempt had been made to decapitate the body. The twenty-one-year-old in custody, Josh Riley, will be charged with murder."

My son? Charged with murder? Panic gnawed at me as air wheezed from my lungs. It couldn't be happening. Not to my family—not to my Josh.

I couldn't take anymore. Grabbing the remote control, I'd turned off the television and dropped down onto the couch, the dusting cloth falling uselessly to the floor. For a moment, I'd struggled to breathe.

Nothing could have made me believe that Josh was capable of murder. But, while Ace and his friends remained at large, he was the one who was going to be blamed. I'd dropped my head and prayed to the God that I had ignored for more years than I'd wanted to remember.

"Please, God, let the police find the others quickly, so that my son can come home," I whispered.

Surely, the police would let Josh go, once they'd realized that he wasn't involved? The tears had started to roll down my face, as I'd had to face the fact that, simply by being there and transporting that man in his father's car, Josh was involved. I'd heard a noise behind me, and had tried to wipe the tears from my eyes as I'd turned around.

It was Becky, Ace's wife. Her eyes were red-rimmed from crying. She'd stood there, wringing her hands and looking at me beseechingly. I couldn't offer her any comfort, though. It was her husband who'd gotten my son into the whole mess.

"I heard from Arnold," she began.

She was the only person I'd ever heard refer to Ace by his real name. Everyone else used his nickname.

"Where is he?" I asked, my voice cold.

"He didn't say. He picked up a new cell phone and told me to go to the local pay phone. Then he called me back there. The odds are that the police have our phone tapped."

"What did he say?" I asked tersely.

"He said it's not as bad as it sounds."

"Oh, Becky, how can it be any worse? I just heard the news. The young man is dead. Your husband walked away and let my son get taken in by the police."

I'd wanted to grab her and shake her until she'd cried for mercy. Or, at least, until she'd admitted that she knew where Ace was. Nothing she'd said could have convinced me that she didn't know.

Becky, and her husband, was close. They did everything together. For a long time, I had tried to turn a blind eye to some of the things that Becky and Ace were doing. I'd known that they both used drugs, but I had allowed myself to believe that it was only marijuana. But I'd never been certain and, as long as they didn't use drugs at my house, I'd always felt that there wasn't anything that I could do about it. There had been a rumor that Ace was involved in dealing, but when I'd asked him about it, he had denied everything.

The police had admitted that the young man who had been killed the night before had been a drug user. Had Ace asked Josh to drive him over there to pick up a drug debt? The more I'd thought about it, the more sense it had made.

"Is Ace going to turn himself in?" I asked Becky, my arms wrapped about myself so that I wouldn't slap her.

"He said the guy is with him and Rex, and that he's alive. They only beat him up."

"Oh, please, Becky, grow up! The police have found the body. That kid was alive when Josh last saw him. He told me that. Ace has to turn himself in and get Josh out of jail."

"Arnold didn't do it. He said it was Rex and Gus. They're the ones who killed him. Anyway, he was worthless. He was a police informant."

"I don't care who, or what, he was. Ace has to give himself up. Until you can tell me that he has, I don't want to see you around here. In case you didn't notice, there's an unmarked police car out there. The police are watching everyone who comes and goes. I suppose they figure that Ace might come around here and ask Glenn to help him." Laughter had bubbled up inside me. "He can't even help his own son. How can he help anyone else?"

Becky had backed out of the room and disappeared. I'd slammed my hand over my mouth to stop the bitter laughter, the sound tinged with hysteria. Then the tears had come again, and I'd dropped down onto the floor. I'd cradled my head in my arms and cried for my poor, frightened son.

The day had worn on and the news was grim. The police wouldn't let us see our son, but I did have a good talk with the lawyer we'd chosen for him. It was the lawyer who'd come up with the idea of contacting the manager of the service station where Josh had stopped to fill up his dad's car. We had an account there. I knew that Josh was between paydays, and wouldn't have had any money.

When we'd talked to the service station manager, he'd handed over the surveillance tapes from that night. There was my son, as clear as day. Finally, we'd had definite proof of where he'd been at 12:30 that night. If only the autopsy had proven that the time of death had been after Josh had left the other men, then I knew that my son would have a chance.

Glenn had calmed down after he'd seen the tape and realized that there was no way that Josh could have been out there, burying a body on the beach. Glenn himself knew what time our son had arrived home that night. Josh had been dragged into something that was not of his making. All he'd been guilty of was giving a friend a ride. Finally, Glenn's anger was focused on Ace. He'd always thought of Ace as a friend. But how could a friend have done something so terrible to us?

The next morning had brought more news. Glenn and I had hovered in front of the television. We were afraid that, if we walked away, we would miss something vital to keeping Josh out of jail.

Ace had turned himself in to the local police. He'd gone on record, stating that Josh Riley had not been there when the young man had been killed. Rex and his friends were still missing, but the police were hoping to bring them into custody before the day was over.

120

"Thank God," I whispered. "Now they'll let Josh come home."

That wasn't the case, though. In fact, they still wouldn't let us see him. He was to be transferred to the nearest correctional center later that day. The police were still charging him with assault, aiding and abetting, and unlawful killing, as opposed to murder. Also, they'd accused him of tampering with a body. The list just had kept getting longer and longer.

The upshot was that they didn't truly believe Ace. The police had decided that Josh still had to carry some of the blame, just because he'd been there. How could I survive, knowing that my son was in jail?

We'd asked the lawyer to apply for bail, but his suggestion had been to wait and see what happened before we headed down that road.

Is this guy for real? I thought. I wanted my son home, as soon as possible. The lawyer told us that it was better if he stayed in jail until the case came to court. He insisted that it was harder for a young man to face going back to jail after the court case. And, he'd made it very clear that Josh would have to spend some time in jail. His biggest focus was to find enough evidence to get the charges reduced as much as possible—to prove that he wasn't responsible for the death of that young man.

Within a week, the police had picked up the other offenders. I'd thought that everything would be okay after that, but it wasn't. Rex, in an effort to save his own skin, had stated that Ace and Josh had killed the young man. Not for one minute did I believe that—not of Josh. It wasn't such a stretch of the imagination to see Ace doing it, but not my baby.

With Josh transferred to the main prison facility, we were able to see him, if only once a week. It took us almost two hours to get there, but it was a drive I was happy to make—if it meant that I could see Josh.

Glenn's hand had gripped mine as we'd approached the front of the prison for the first time and registered our names. Then we were ushered inside and given a locker in which to place all of our personal belongings. We were to bring nothing inside with us.

"I don't know why they bother," I whispered to Glenn. "They won't let us have a contact visit this time, anyway."

My hands were shaking as I'd stood in line with Glenn and ten other people while the warden had walked a drug dog up and down the line. I was made to feel like a criminal, when all I'd wanted to do was to see my son. Finally, they'd cleared us to enter the visiting area.

Because the first visit was always a non-contact visit, Glenn and I were led into a glass cage. We'd seated ourselves at the table in the center of the room. Another glass panel had divided the table in half.

It was high enough that it was impossible to reach over it.

Within minutes, Josh came into the room and sat down on the other side of the glass. I'd flattened my hand on the glass and cried when Josh had placed his palm over mine on the other side. I'd wanted to touch him so badly, to feel for myself that he was all right.

His face was covered in bruises, as if he'd been beaten. His eyes looked puffy, but he'd still managed to smile. He'd leaned forward and put his mouth up near the grill in the center of the glass panel.

"Hi, Mom," he whispered. "I'm so sorry about this." His eyes were filled with tears.

"It's okay, Josh. I know you didn't do it. And so does your father. Don't you, Glenn?" I'd elbowed Glenn in the ribs.

"We'll find a way to get you home, son," Glenn promised. "We've got the best lawyer that we could find. He'll help us."

"How are we going to pay for a lawyer?" Josh asked.

Glenn had cleared his throat. "I haven't talked to your mother about this yet, but I thought that we could sell the house."

At his father's words, Josh had really started to cry—great, shuddering sobs that shook his frame.

"I'm sorry. I don't want you to have to sell your home," he said brokenly.

"No, Josh. Your father is right," I insisted. "The house has to go. Home is wherever we make it. It has nothing to do with a building. And, anyway, when you get out, I'd rather that you didn't come back to that house. I think it would be a good idea if you started fresh. So don't be upset, okay?"

The time flew past and before we knew it, we were being ushered out of the correctional facility. I'd cried all the way home, because I'd missed being able to hug my Josh.

Glenn seemed to have aged in that visit—softened, somehow. He was more considerate of my feelings and me, and insisted on helping out more around the house.

The weeks had dragged on without change. We'd spent time with the lawyer, going through the police brief and trying to come up with a defense for Josh.

On top of that, we'd had to get the house ready to go on the market. Glenn had helped me with the painting, cleaning, and the maintenance jobs—all the little jobs that people put off, figuring that they'd get around to it later, but never did. I'd started to sort out fifteen years of accumulated junk and was deciding what we wanted to take with us when we moved.

And every weekend, we drove to the correctional facility to see our son. It broke my heart to see the changes in him. He had become angry and bitter regarding his friendship with Ace. In fact, I believed he'd blamed his father for bringing Ace into the house for the first time, all those years before.

I'd never seen Becky again, although I did hear from our lawyer that my suspicions had been correct: Ace was a drug dealer. Becky had taken over his business, running drugs to make money, instead of going out and getting a job like any normal person would have done. She had disregarded my warning about the police watching us and had set up her business in her own home, just one street away from our house.

One Sunday morning, only a few weeks later, the police had conducted a dawn raid and had caught her with a large quantity of drugs on the premises—enough to charge her with supplying. So now she, too, was in jail, and her children were living with her sister. It was the kids that I felt sorry for, with both of their parents in jail. And I'd since learned that it was Ace's second murder charge. He had already done time.

Finally, it was time for the court case. Glenn had held my hand as we'd walked into the courtroom. We'd sat up the front, where we could be as near as possible to Josh. His skin looked pallid, evidence of the fact that he didn't get much sun. His shoulders were broader, and his arms bulged with muscle. He'd spent a lot of time inside working out with weights. It was a way for him to deal with some of the anger that was festering inside of him.

Each of the men was dealt with separately. Each had his own lawyer to defend him. When the prosecutor had read out the charges against Josh, I'd cringed. I'd glanced across the courtroom at the parents of the boy who had been murdered. His mother looked tired, and his father had kept his head bowed. They'd looked like good people, although the brother was mouthy enough to get himself thrown out of the courtroom because he wouldn't keep quiet.

When they'd put Josh on the stand, I'd hung on his every word, convinced that the jury just had to find him innocent. He was my baby. How could anyone have believed him capable of anything as heinous as murder?

The jury didn't see it my way, though. At the end of the trial, Josh was sentenced to four years in jail for his part in the whole fiasco. My sweet boy wouldn't be coming home with me. Glenn had walked me from the courthouse, with tears rolling down my face.

"Let's go home, love," he said gently.

When we'd arrived back at the house that we'd been renting, Glenn had looked drained and weary. His heart had been giving him a bit of trouble recently and he'd had to increase his medication. Our other son, Bryce, had moved out into his own place. He'd told us that he was tired of all the notoriety we'd had over Josh's involvement in the murder. So the house was as quiet as a graveyard.

I'd patted Glenn on the cheek. "Go upstairs and lie down, sweetie. You look exhausted."

"What about you?" he asked. "You're taking it pretty well, but I'm still worried about you."

"I think I'll sit down here in the family room for a while," I told him. "I need some time to myself. Maybe I'll go out and do some gardening—burn off those hedge clippings from last week."

"It always did soothe you, didn't it? Gardening, I mean," Glenn murmured. He'd climbed up the staircase wearily and headed for bed.

I'd waited until I could no longer hear any noise from upstairs. Then I'd opened the closet in the corner of the family room and pulled out a brown paper packet before heading out to the backyard.

Taking the lid off the incinerator, I'd fed in the dried hedge clippings until the container was almost full. With a quick glance over my shoulder, I'd emptied the brown paper packet onto the top of the clippings.

A soft green shirt fell out. It was the shirt that I had bought Josh for his last birthday—the same one he'd been wearing when he'd left to go and drive Ace to Medford.

I'd stared at it, fixated. Then I couldn't help myself: I'd had to check it again. Lifting it by the collar, I'd spread it out over the top of the incinerator. The entire front of the shirt was covered with blood, much more blood than would have come from a cut eye and a bloody nose.

The shirt had been stashed under a rock in the garden of the old house. I'd found it when I'd started to clean up in preparation for the sale. Somehow, the police had missed it in their search. So I had hidden it and carried it from the old house over to the one we were renting. Now that the court case was over, I knew that it was time to get rid of it.

Glenn had wondered why I was taking it so well. I'd grimaced as I'd shoved the shirt among the garden refuse and flicked a lighter to set it aflame. Then I'd stood and watched as it had disintegrated into ash.

Glenn would have been horrified if he'd known about the shirt. He had formed a new bond with Josh, even though Josh was in jail. I didn't want to shatter that relationship. So I'd burned the evidence.

Why had I been taking things so well? Because, although I could never have been convinced that Josh had taken part in the murder, he'd definitely been there when it had taken place. The shirt had proven that. But there was no way that I would say anything about it—to the police, or to anyone else. I loved my son. I couldn't turn him in.

The courts had handed down his punishment. He'd always hated being hemmed in, but he'd do the hard time. And when he came out, his father and I would be there, waiting for him. We'd help him put together his life. And for the first time, I felt as though Glenn would be a real father to him.

And me? What's my punishment for my silence? I have signed up to work as a counselor at a youth camp for children with drug problems. Perhaps by helping someone else's child, I will be able to atone for my own sins.

THE END

www.ingramcontent.com/pod-product-compliance
Lightning Source LLC
Chambersburg PA
CBHW071358170626
46811CB00003B/1173